The Weeping Sands

John Wheatley

Silversea Books

Copyright © 2012 John Wheatley

All rights reserved

The Weeping Sands is a work of historical fiction. Some incidents and characters are drawn from historical records but their realisation is essentially imaginative.

No part of this book may be reproduced, or stored in a retrieval system, or transmitted in any form or by any means, electronic, mechanical, photocopying, recording, or otherwise, without express written permission of the publisher.

ISBN: 9781475063608

Contents

Title Page	
Copyright	
Part 1	1
Chapter 1	3
Chapter 2	7
Chapter 3	9
Chapter 4	12
Chapter 5	15
Chapter 6	19
Chapter 7	23
Chapter 8	26
Chapter 9	29
Chapter 10	32
Chapter 11	34
Chapter 12	36
Chapter 13	40
Chapter 14	44
Chapter 15	49
Chapter 16	50
Chapter 17	52

Part 2	56
Chapter 18	57
Chapter 19	61
Chapter 20	64
Chapter 21	65
Chapter 22	69
Chapter 23	73
Chapter 24	76
Chapter 25	77
Chapter 26	83
Chapter 27	87
Chapter 28	90
Chapter 29	95
Chapter 30	98
Chapter 31	102
Chapter 32	104
Chapter 33	109
Chapter 34	115
Chapter 35	117
Chapter 36	120
Chapter 37	122
Chapter 38	124
Chapter 39	127
Chapter 40	131
Chapter 41	134
Chapter 42	138
Chapter 43	145
Part 3	147

Chapter 44	148
Chapter 45	155
Chapter 46	165
Chapter 47	167
Chapter 48	168
Chapter 49	170
Chapter 50	173
Chapter 51	178
Chapter 52	185
Chapter 53	190
Chapter 54	193
Chapter 55	196
Chapter 56	199
Chapter 57	207
Chapter 58	209
Chapter 59	215
Chapter 60	218
Chapter 61	221
Chapter 62	224
Chapter 63	227
Chapter 64	230
Chapter 65	231
Chapter 66	235
ABOUT THE AUTHOR	242
johnwheatley@ymail.com	243

Part 1

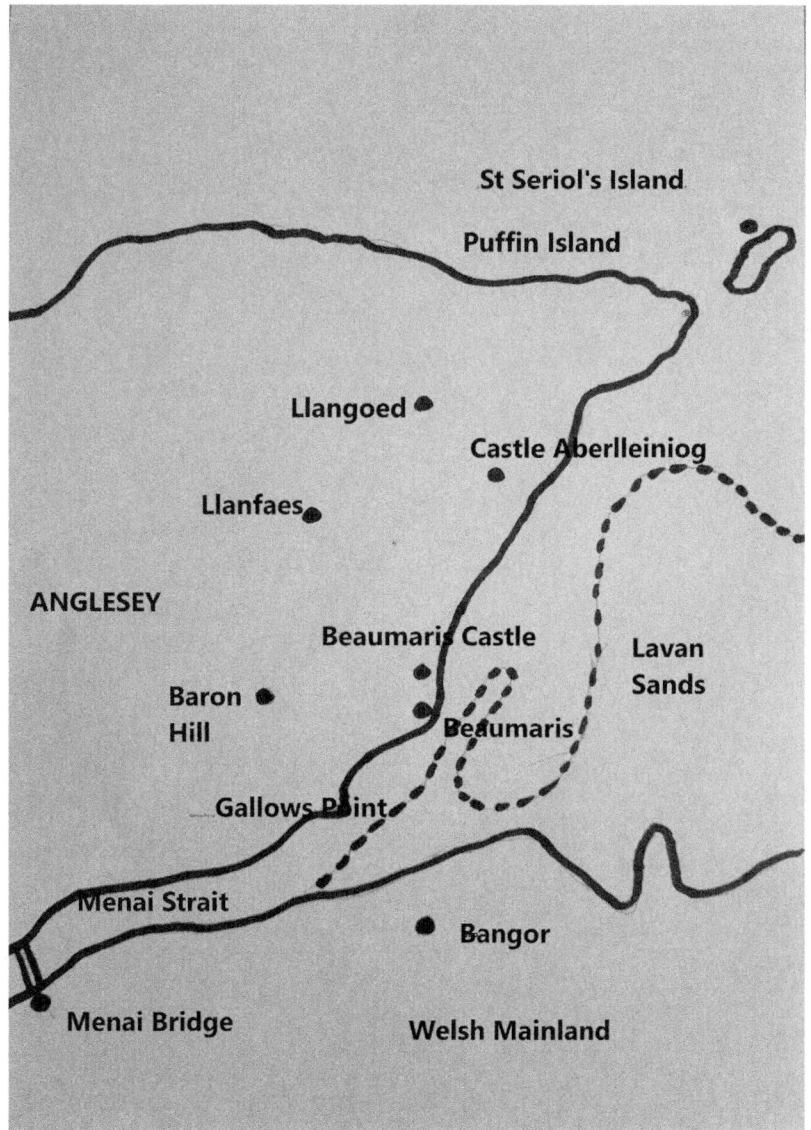

JOHN WHEATLEY

Chapter 1

17th September 1831

The Lavan Sands disappeared before us in a swirling sea-mist. The opposite shore, at Beaumaris, our destination, clearly visible at the start of the journey from Conway, was now obscure. The prospect before us was dismal, and yet Mr Hughes, our coachman from Chester, having spoken to the guide at Penmaenmawr, insisted that this was our best means of crossing to the Anglesey shore before daylight faded. The alternative, he pointed out, entailed a further drive of six miles to the new toll bridge at Bangor, and then a four-mile return from Porthaethwy to Beaumaris.

My sister Isobel was indisposed this morning, after a sleepless night, and that was the reason for the delay of our departure from Conway.

Venturing onto the sands, we found them firm and even, and made good progress, coming opposite the ferry on the Anglesey shore after little more than half an hour. Our luggage transferred to the ferryboat, we bade farewell to Mr Hughes, who appeared to be in no small haste to be on his way, and began our crossing of the channel, which was half a mile wide at the state of the tide when we came to it. The ferryman told us that the licence for the crossing has been in his family for six generations, but his business has been greatly diminished by the new Menai Bridge, and he foresees a time soon when the ferry will be used only by those whose trade is with the shellfish with which the surrounding sandbanks and shelves are plentifully supplied.

Our journey to Baron Hill was completed by a short drive

through the village, and we are grateful to Sir Richard Bulkeley, who had made arrangements from London, for his household to be in readiness for our arrival. My sister, who had grown agitated during the latter stages of our crossing of the Lavan Sands, retired to bed soon after our arrival, and I, too, tired after four days of travel, having spent this last hour bringing my diary up to date, am now ready for rest.

18th September 1831

Our host, Sir Richard, the tenth Baronet, is presently in London, and we are unlikely to see him for several weeks as his business keeps him there through most of the autumn. Our connections with the Bulkeley family are tenuous, going back several generations on our mother's side to a relative who was married to someone of the Bulkeley line, but hearing of my sister's recent difficulties, Sir Richard was gracious enough to offer Baron Hill, remote as it is from the distractions and tribulations of the capital, as a place suitable for convalescence and recuperation.

I should explain.

During the spring of this year my sister formed a most unfortunate liaison. The man concerned, James Pennington, an artist, was engaged to paint her portrait, and it seems that during the sittings arranged for that purpose, an attachment was formed in which my sister's affections were cruelly exploited. So far advanced were the clandestine plans agreed upon between them – for no proper relationship could be sanctioned between parties of such disparate social standing, and this they knew – that my sister had been discovered missing from Evesham Place for more than twelve hours before the couple were apprehended at Dartford, apparently en route for the Kentish coast and elopement in France.

It was, of course, quite natural that the family should hold James Pennington accountable for the deterioration in my sister's health which followed these events, but Doctor Fairhurst, though by no means excusing that young man's behaviour, was firmly of the opinion that the decisions taken by my sister – to follow a course of action that would alienate her forever from her family and those of her own class, to link herself to an impecunious artist, to chain herself to an uncertain life of poverty and degradation, amidst the known immorality of many of those with whom she must mix, already denoted a mental condition that was seriously out of balance with nature.

Her condition is one which renders her prone to extreme changes of mood, sometimes to profound melancholy, and sleeplessness, sometimes to excitability; sometimes to imaginings in which the stuff of dreams and nightmares seems to become a waking reality.

However, I am in great hope that the tranquillity and beauty of this place will provide the tonic needed to restore her spirits. No description of mine can match the splendour of Baron Hill. Set above the town, it commands an open view of the changing panorama of the Welsh mountains beyond.

My mother was unfortunate in both her marriages. My father, a nephew of the Earl of Duxbury, contracted a fever in the American colonies, and died there even before I was born. Her second husband, Isobel's father, was killed in the fighting at Salamanca, and the Hall at Flixbury Manor, where we lived, passed by inheritance to his younger brother who was kind enough to let us remain in residence there until my mother's death eight years later, when I was twelve and Isobel ten. After that, we became wards of Mr Harcourt, my mother's cousin, by the terms of her will, and our domestic and financial arrangements fell to his charge.

Though born each of a different father, we were brought up entirely as sisters, both taking the surname, Harcourt, my mother's maiden name, and the fact that I had never known my father, and that Isobel had no clear memory of hers, meant that no invidious comparisons were ever drawn, nor did any rivalries exist between us as is sometimes the case with siblings of different parentage.

Thankfully, I have a small annuity which was left to me in

trust by my father, and when she reaches her age of maturity, Isobel will inherit a portion of her own father's legacy, which includes twenty acres of land near Flixbury, and an income of £2,000 per annum, so that we may both hope to live in reasonable independence, though, as my guardian, Mr Harcourt, explained, Isobel's prospective wealth might well make her a target for men of questionable motives, and, in this respect, it was even more important to protect her from the attentions of Mr Pennington.

The house here, we are informed, dates back to the time of the first King James, though it was greatly modified in the last century and adapted in the Palladian style by Samuel Wyatt. It was at this time also that the formal gardens were laid out.

The town of Beaumaris was defended during the civil war. The town was strongly for the king, but the forces were defeated not far from here by the Parliamentary army led by General Thomas Mytton whose men were billeted in the town. It is said that one of the Beaumaris men, a Thomas Cheadle secretly had conference with the Parliament men to gain advantage for himself.

The fortification here, though seemingly less imposing and warlike than others to be found in Wales is much praised for its formal beauty and symmetry. There is another castle, some two miles distant, we have been informed, and to which, it is proposed, we take an outing in suitable weather, which is greatly dilapidated and overgrown, with only the rampart and a broken tower to identify it. It is known to some of the local people as Lady Cheadle's fort

But poor Sir Richard! His own life has not been without tragedy. Having succeeded to the estate in the summer of 1827, his happiness seemed complete when he was married the following year to Charlotte Hughes, dear Charlotte whom we met twice at Bath before she was married, and who was truly the sweetest of creatures. And then, before another year was out, poor Sir Richard was in mourning for his new bride. Such is the terrible uncertainty of life.

Chapter 2

Jenna Shaw, children's TV presenter of the 1990s and member, more recently, of the BBC's *Country Retreats* team, received a telephone call, one Friday morning, from her agent, Rebecca Weissman.

"I've had a call from Simon Black's P.A. They want you to consider being on *What's my Lineage*."

"What, the ancestors thingy?"

"Yes."

"Not certain about that, Bex, don't really like, you know, things that are too personal."

"You'll be on National TV for an hour, just you, yourself and no-one else but you. Think of the exposure!"

Jenna had finished the latest series of *Country Retreats*, and another was due to start in the spring, but you could never be certain. It was all too easy for a TV presenter to slip down the ladder into obscurity.

"At least it's not *Celebrity Big Brother*."

"God, you're right!"

She telephoned Simon Black, the producer.

"How does it work?"

"Have you ever seen it?"

"Yes, I saw the Miles Brinstock one a couple of months ago."

Miles Brinstock, the ever-so-well-bred drama critic had discovered that his great grandmother probably worked the streets of Liverpool in the early years of the last century.

"Ah, yes, the Miles Brinstock one! Well, you've got some idea of the format. Of course, we do a lot of preliminary work first, just to see, you know, if it'll work as a show."

Jenna was sufficiently aware of the media world to know that there was no such thing as reality, only what could be converted into a show with its own narrative.

"You do some research, I suppose."

"First off, yes. Then a mutual decision, go ahead or kill it. If it's a yes, we hand it onto you and a camera crew. We set up all the contacts, of course."

"And then you edit it."

"Then we edit it."

"Do I have to have skeletons in the closet?"

"Not necessarily, though it does help. Have you, by the way?"

"Got any skeletons? I don't think so."

"Well, never mind, darling. You can't have everything."

"But I suppose it could be completely dull."

"Well it could be. But unlikely. Unless people stayed in the same village for generation after generation. But a lot of people moved at some point, and the reasons for movement usually throw up something interesting."

"Right."

"Anyway, Jenna, look, why don't you come in and have a chat."

"OK."

"I'll get Maisie to set it up. Maisie's the PA by the way."

"OK."

Chapter 3

1644

It was common knowledge, at least amongst those who faced the truth, that the king would lose Chester. A series of assaults and sieges, led by Sir William Brereton, commander of the Parliamentary men in Cheshire, had weakened the defences and demoralised both troops and people. The efforts of Sir Nicholas Byron, the promises of intervention from Prince Rupert, and Prince Maurice, even the King himself, had only served to delay the inevitable. As Thomas Cheadle passed through the town, accompanied by his son, Richard, on their way from Stockport to Beaumaris on the island of Anglesey, the evidence of war's depredation was everywhere to be seen, not only in the breached fortifications and the burnt out ruins of houses struck by flaming mortars, but in the faces of the people, accustomed to peace and prosperity, now shocked into familiarity with hunger, deprivation and disease.

"When Chester goes," said Thomas Cheadle, as they passed through the Handbridge Gate, "the north of Wales will go next."

"Is that why Chester is important?" said Richard, who despite the turbulent world he was seeing, was enjoying his first journey away from his grandfather's home.

"To us, yes, maybe."

"Grandfather said that the whole of Anglesey's for the king."

"The whole of Wales. But Chester's the route to Ireland, too, and to the North. The king needs Chester."

"What will they do? On Anglesey, I mean?"

"That," said Thomas Cheadle, "we shall have to see."

The young man did not understand the causes of the war.

There were some who spoke of the misdemeanours of the king and his abuse of privilege, some who spoke of the wickedness of the Catholic church and the Laudian bishops, the need for freedom of worship and freedom of conscience, but most of the people he knew leaned neither one way nor the other, or simply went along with a family loyalty or gave their support to some tradition of the neighbourhood. All feared the power of war to spill blood and destroy livelihoods; few seemed to believe that life would be better when the war was over.

During the battle of Castle Hill, in Stockport, he had supported Prince Rupert, partly because he had seen him ride by on horseback and he seemed such a dashing figure, and partly because his grandfather said Prince Rupert and his father stood for the same cause, but he had been thrilled also by tales of the exploits of the 'Manchester Men', which seemed a brave title to have achieved, and they were definitely for Parliament.

"Practise your swordsmanship," his grandfather had advised him, "then whoever stands against you will know he has met his match!"

It was advice he had tried to follow, and now, at nineteen, though slight of build, rather more like his mother than his father, they said, he carried his sword proudly at his hilt and felt he could give a good account of himself in any skirmish that might occur.

To the south of Chester, the road took them towards Mold and Shotton. Even in the smaller towns and villages, the discord of war was evident. Rapacious local officials seeking profit from the power their authority gave them; the people surly, hostile, suspicious; soldiers, given free quarter instead of pay, a dangerous rabble, intent on plunder, their cause, if they ever had any true sense of it, lost in the scramble for survival.

They stayed that night at an inn in St Asaph. At the entrance to the town, a parcel of ruffians, probably deserters, eyed them menacingly, but seeing they carried weapons, grinned cynically and stood off, letting them pass; Thomas Cheadle had the look of a man who would not readily be interfered with.

The following day they came to the ferry at Conway in the mid-afternoon, and continued, despite the onset of bitter weather, towards the rugged bulk of Penmaenmawr. The outline of Anglesey was just visible in a smudge of rain, three miles off across the waters of the estuary. The castle of Beaumaris, set low against the hillside was not distinguishable from this distance. Empty and abandoned for two hundred years, an ivy clad ruin, it was Cheadle himself who, as Deputy Constable under Lord Dorset, had refurbished the fortification, and raised a garrison of eighty men to defend it for the king when the need arose, though even then his motives had been doubted and questioned.

But that was of no account now. The times were changing. Chester would fall, and then the test would come, and men would have to change with the times, or fall, too.

He narrowed his eyes against the sharp salt wind.

The tide was turning, the darkness falling. They would need to hurry to catch the ferry before the channel grew too wide.

What would be, would be. Cheadle himself was ready to look at any possibility.

He was a man who had lived with unpopularity and cared about it not at all.

A man who had loved another man's wife.

A man who had stood trial for murder.

He did not intend to fall now.

The sound of the horses' hooves thundered on the sand as they galloped, into the teeth of the wind, across the Lavan Sands towards the ferry at Llanfaes.

Chapter 4

The offices of *Sunrise Productions* were in Lavender Street, a short walk from Pelham Circus tube station. It was a converted warehouse, which was also the storage depot of a separate company dealing in furniture and props for film and television.

The building was dingy, with peeling paint and dirty windows, and with a general air of grubby confusion. It reminded Jenna of her first experience of television – not in some glorious citadel with beautiful people, but in back rooms looking out on brick walls, buildings with absolutely no character at all, industrial estates, dingy bars – it was one thing about media people that they seemed to like the dingiest, dirtiest and dodgiest of places to meet for social purposes.

"Don't expect it to be glamorous," Angus Robbs, her first producer had said to her. "Ninety per cent of what you see on TV is pure illusion; the other ten percent is downright lies!"

"Hi, Jenna Shaw."

"Yes," said the girl at the desk, with the tone of recognition to which Jenna had grown familiar. Most people had seen her on *Country Retreats*, some even remembered her from the rather frivolous kids' programme with which she'd started her career, *Switch Swivel and Swatch*. The girl at the desk had dark bobbed hair, a pale blue satin blouse, pink lip-gloss and nails, and an air of neatness which seemed completely at odds with the apparent disorganisation of the office around her.

"Lovely to meet you. I'm Maisie. Maisie Flood."

"Hi Maisie."

"So, anyway, take a seat. Shall I organise some coffee or are you…?

She trailed off, puckering her nose, as if she was aware that there might be a category of people who objected to being offered coffee.

"No," said Jenna. "No thanks. Later perhaps, depending on… how long do you think we'll be…?"

"An hour maybe, I just need to… is that OK?" she said, giggling slightly, as if not knowing how much of the obvious she needed to state.

"Fine."

"Right, then. Well, you've had a quick word with Simon, I guess he gave you the basics."

"Well, yes, basically, I suppose."

"Right, well what we do now, and I'll just get a pad and make a couple of notes if that's OK, is just get some background, so that we can plan the script."

"Script, is it as formal as that?"

Maisie laughed and pouted. "It's not really very formal."

It was at that moment that the coin dropped. She's gay, said Jenna to herself.

During the four years of *Switch and Swatch* Jenna had been seriously advised to keep her own sexual orientation under wraps. *We want the teenage boys to have a bit of a crush on you, that's part of the formula, don't want them getting confused.* She had, at that stage, not come out, not officially, anyway, and so she played along. It was her first job in television. She didn't want to antagonise anybody.

"So, tell me a bit about your family."

"Right, well, my dad was an American."

"Was, is he…?"

"Dead, yes."

"Sorry."

"It was a car crash when I was seventeen. My first year at university."

"How sad. What did he do?"

"He was in advertising."

"But your mum's…?"

"Alive, yes."

"I was going to say English!" said Maisie with the little tinkle of self-deprecatory laughter that Jenna was beginning to find distinctly and a little disconcertingly attractive.

"Yes. Yes. Very English and very alive."

"Right," said Maisie, half an hour later, "what we do now is, we get our little eager beavers from research on the case, and they do their digging about, and basically we see what we can come up with based on what you've told me. Then I'll call you in about four weeks. In the meantime, if you can sort of let your mum know, and we'll get someone to call round to see her, to look at family albums, that sort of thing, does that sound OK?"

"Yes."

"I was an avid Switch and Swatcher," said Maisie at the door.

"You poor thing," said Jenna, her characteristic response to such admissions. She tried to picture Maisie, as a thirteen- or fourteen-year-old, listening to that ridiculous and irritating jingle.

Don't forget, don't forget, don't forget to watch,
Switch Swivel and Swatch.

"Will I be seeing you? As part of the programme, I mean?"

"Oh, yes," said Maisie, briskly, and a little more professionally than Jenna had hoped for.

Chapter 5

22nd September 1831

Our accommodation here is very comfortable. The great staircase leads from the hall to the state apartments – the house has frequently received guests of the highest rank – and a second stairway leads off from this to a group of rooms at the rear of the house, which at one time, we are told, was a nursery adjacent to the master and mistress' suite, though the house underwent significant changes in the last century, and the rooms are now used for lesser guests such as ourselves, though they are spacious and very pleasant.

Behind us, and to each side of the house – by contrast to the splendour of the great open panorama which forms the view from the front – we are surrounded by dense woodland. How far this forest extends I do not know, but in my own imagination it goes on as far as the unknown may be thought to go, and I imagine it full of wild creatures, which is dreadful to think of, especially at night.

The household, during Sir Richard's absence, is not extensive. Sir Richard's valet, Leyton, and his butler, Mr Roberts attend him at Cavendish Square, St Marylebone, as does his housekeeper, Mrs Prine. George Thomas, who has lived on the estate all his life – he is now somewhere near fifty – is the husbandman and gardener, and his wife Jane acts as the housekeeper and mistress over the other female servants in Mrs Prine's absence. Their daughter, another Jane, and Margaret Jones, both girls of about fifteen, and Thomas Coates, a young man of twenty-five [somewhat moody and taciturn] makes up the retinue. Others from the village, up to a hundred men we are told, are hired on the land of the estate when the season requires it, and when Sir Richard is in residence, a host of additional servants is taken on, laundry-maids, footmen, pantry-boys, kitchen-maids, grooms, chambermaids. In a town of this size, it is easy to see how important a role such a house as Baron Hill plays in local matters.

25th September 1831

At breakfast this morning, Isobel looked pale and drawn, almost haggard. Her face had a pallid lustre, scarcely more alive than alabaster, and her eyes were deeply shadowed; all this, together with her dishevelled hair was a sight which I would well have wished not to be on display for the benefit of the servants.

"We are guests, here," I said to her. "We must strive to avoid creating an unfavourable impression."

"I'm sorry," she said, vaguely. "I didn't sleep well."

"Isobel, that is no excuse for neglecting your…"

"I heard noises," she said, cutting across my warning, "in the middle of the night."

"What sort of noises?"

"At first I didn't know if I was asleep or awake, but then…"

"What sort of noises?" I insisted.

"It was in the room," she said now looking at me directly for the first time.

"Isobel, what noise did you imagine you heard?"

"It sounded like someone in distress."

"Distress!" I said, now thoroughly alarmed.

"But I didn't imagine it, Emily. It was real."

I immediately summoned the parlour maid and instructed her to request Mrs Thomas, the housekeeper, to attend us at our rooms. In fact, it was Thomas Coates who knocked on the door of Isobel's chamber, some ten minutes later.

"Mrs Thomas is in the village," he said. "What's the trouble?"

"My sister heard sounds in the night. It disturbed her sleep."

He nodded his head slightly, the nearest he might come to an acknowledgment.

"Is it possible that any of the servants could have been in this part of the house, during the night?" I continued.

"The servants' quarters are on the other side of the house," he said. "What did you hear?"

"It sounded like someone in distress," I said, repeating Isobel's description."

He looked from me to Isobel.

"That's what you said, isn't it?"

"Yes," said Isobel, now seeming uncertain of herself. "I think… it seemed like distress."

"It was a voice you heard, then?"

"Yes, a woman's voice."

Two chamber maids who were at their work in the room, catching each other's eyes, could not prevent themselves from a snort of laughter at this point, though when they saw my look of admonition, they quickly desisted.

"Where did it come from?" he asked, a little impatiently.

"It seemed to be inside the room?" said Isobel, before I could stop her.

"Inside the room? Perhaps we have ghosts in the house, then!"

"I insist you take this seriously!" I said, in defence of Isobel, though I rather feared we were both now drawing the same conclusion, that Isobel's overwrought imagination had invented the entire episode. "Are there any other rooms, adjacent to these?"

He opened the other doors on the corridor, but each in turn proved to be merely a linen cupboard or store of some other sort.

"What is on the other side of that wall? Over there."

"Over there? That's an outside wall, miss. There's nothing on the other side of that besides fresh air."

"And there is no other access to this part of the house other than the second staircase?"

He shook his head. "It seems likely to me," he said, at last, "that what you heard, miss, was a cat. You'll often see them sitting on the ledges outside, and they make strange noises, sometimes, almost human."

Isobel furrowed her brow and seemed unconvinced, but I decided that this was a suitable note on which to end the conversation.

"Thank you, Mr Coates. That will be all."

Isobel sat for some time, in a distant and abstracted mood, but a short walk around the garden, later in the morning, however, brought some colour back to her cheeks, and she seemed in a more settled frame of mind.

"How beautiful it is here!" she said, as if noting it for the first time. We were standing on the terrace with the full view of the mountains before us, and the surrounding trees were in their full autumn splendour. "I think I will do some sketching here. Do you think Thomas will set up our easels here this afternoon?"

She did not wait for a reply but walked on so quickly that I had to hurry to catch up with her on the flight of stone steps which led down to the lower terrace and the formal gardens.

Chapter 6

1623

A rare spring morning, the air as sweet as clover to the taste.

In the ivy-clad ramparts of Beaumaris Castle, nesting swallows make a busy fuss. Across the Menai Strait, mirror still, the mountains rise imperiously, slate grey in the clear morning light.

Thomas Cheadle, standing on the shore at Fryars, watches the approach of the ferry which is to carry Sir Richard, and his son, across the narrow channel to the Lavan Sands. The oars dip noiselessly into the water, and just a watery ripple is heard as the boat's prow noses forward. The horses, now a little impatient, and nervous of the crossing, which they remember, play with the points of their hoofs in the pebbles and sand of the shore.

Sir Richard is travelling to London, as he does twice a year, for though, unlike his father, he has chosen not to play a direct part in the affairs of Parliament, he likes to make it his business to mix with those who do, and to live the while in town. The son, aged twelve, is going to Thavies, a school linked to the Inns of Court. The family has property in Marylebone, and part of the household has been sent on before to prepare. Sometimes, Lady Anne and the children accompany Sir Richard to London, but as their father has been saying, on the way to the ferry, the girls are at an age when they become quickly restless in town, and their mother dislikes the city's noise and bustle.

"But you must come with me, Thomas, perhaps when I next go, in the autumn. The life of London is interesting to a young man. You will find much to amuse and entertain you."

"Yes, Sir Richard. Gladly."

"Listen, Thomas. You've been here now, what, four months? Your father served mine for many years, there wasn't a man he trusted more, and I think you're just the fellow to pick up the mantle…"

The ferryman, now ready, called before he could complete making his point.

"Look I'll be brief. What I mean is that I'd like you to consider becoming my secretary. The estate is growing, I need someone to manage things. Consider it. I'll provide you with an office at the hall, and accommodation. Or you can keep up the house in the town if you wish, bring your family here, whatever suits you."

"Ferry away!"

"I'll have to go. Or we'll get stuck in the quicksand, but consider it, Thomas."

"I will."

"Give it your best thought."

"Yes, Sir Richard."

He watched as Sir Richard and his valet, Jenkin, boarded, and helped to urge the horses into the water behind; twenty minutes later, on the sandbank opposite, the horses were shaking the water from their coats. Then they were brought to stand, saddled and girthed, and held steady as Sir Richard and Jenkin mounted. Soon they were tiny figures, lessening into the distance until at last they were lost to sight in the shadow of Penmaenmawr.

Thomas Cheadle remounted his own horse and turned him from the shore. The hoofs clattered on the stones, as the horse, now eager, tried to run on, but Cheadle quickly reined him back to a walk.

Rather than return to the town, or the estate at Baron Hill – for in Sir Richard's absence, there was no pressing business to pursue - he continued along the coast track, towards Penmon and Priestsholme.

On his first visit to Anglesey, the previous autumn, he had driven a herd of pigs from Cheshire, bringing them safely across the Menai Strait at Porthaethwy and thence to the Bulkeley estate. It was no mean feat, for pigs are wilful nimble creatures, not slow and biddable like cattle, and you had to keep your eye on them all the time, night and day. Grateful for this, Sir Richard had given him other work on the estate, errands of responsibility, and had rewarded him amply. He had taken the lease of a small house in the town and had a manservant and housekeeper. Quick-witted, he had picked up the language quite easily, and already spoke better Welsh than Sir Richard, who always said, in his affable and languid way, that he had never really had very much use for it.

There was, in himself, he acknowledged, an energy and restlessness of ambition. Amongst those he spoke with at home, in Stockport, there was talk of young men going abroad, to the new colonies of America, where fortunes were to be made, it was said, on cotton and tobacco plantations. Now there was Sir Richard's offer of a more formal position, one which would make it possible for him to establish himself. It had to be considered.

He rode on for three miles along the coastal track, until it turned sharply to the right to follow the course of a babbling stream running through a sandy meadow towards the sea. On the opposite side of the stream, a steep bank rose, densely wooded, its branches a thick tangle just beginning to show the purple of new buds. Beyond the trees, set on the hillside, was the ancient earth rampart of Aberlleiniog, and it was to this that Thomas Cheadle now directed his horse.

He continued to the hamlet of Lleiniog and then took the track leading up the hill to the earthwork. Overgrown with grass and bramble, there was s strong smell of wood fungus and wild garlic. He walked the horse to the highest part of the rampart, and looked out, over the water to Great Orme's Head and the estuary of the River Conwy. The fortress reached back into a time of which he knew nothing, a past as misty and impenetrable as the sea fog which sometimes drifted into the Menai Strait, and across the island, and it fascinated him. The local people had stories, mostly of the gruesome sort, about the place, but there were no records, and all one could tell was that it must have been prepared for use in some now long forgotten struggle.

It would be possible, Cheadle speculated, looking down from the rampart, to have the site cleared, and build a house there, a fortified house possibly, guarding the eastern flank of the island. Would that satisfy his ambition? It fired his imagination, though perhaps the thought was frivolous.

He rode on, now following the track uphill to the village of Llangoed and then made his way to Llanfaes and Baron Hill.

The Great House at Baron Hill had been built by Sir Richard's father, to provide hospitality for Prince Henry when he became Lord Protector of Ireland. But the Prince died, and it was his younger brother, Charles, who was now heir to the throne of England. There were half a dozen families of wealth and influence on the island, each with its own seat, but Baron Hill was pre-eminent.

In the meadow, at the front of the house, Lady Anne, with her two small daughters, Ann and Mary, was gathering flowers.

"Look, it's Thomas," cried Ann, running towards him, expecting to be picked up and thrown into the air. The girl was open in her affections, full of spirit and laughter.

"Richard has gone to London to become a great lawyer. And father's gone with him. We shall miss them, shan't we mother?"

"We shall."

"Will you come and help us be merry, Thomas?"

"We've been picking flowers," said Mary, more formally. "It's meadow-sweet. We're going to dry it then use it to strew the floor."

"The scent is exquisite," said Lady Anne. She held the flowers forward, and Thomas Cheadle bowed his head. The flowers were creamy white, tightly clustered. The scent was heavily sweet, charged with honey and musk. When he looked up and exchanged glances, the faint curl of a smile, the look in her eyes, seemed to penetrate the depths of his being.

He rode away with chaos in his soul.

Chapter 7

The following day, Thomas Cheadle returned to his family home in Cheshire. His wife, Sarah, five months with child, was a goodly size, but easily tired and prone to sickness.

"You must come with me," he said to her. "I have it in mind to build a home there."

"When the child is born."

"What home?" interjected his father.

"At Aberlleiniog."

"Aberlleiniog? Why, it's a ruin. Not even a ruin. It's an overgrown ditch!"

"It's a foundation. It takes imagination to see it as a fine house, I agree, but it can be done."

"Why don't you stay, try to make your way here?" his father said, later, when they were alone.

"The same reason you didn't. Two brothers and six cousins who would do the same on the same land."

"Well, that's true."

"Besides, you did well enough on Anglesey, didn't you?"

"Well enough. If I had my time again, though, I'd go to Virginia, or Massachusetts."

"And so might I, yet. And then you'll see little enough of your new grandson."

The old man grew silent.

"She has a hard time of it, Sarah," he said at last.

"Yes."

"So your mother says and she knows about these things, but she's young and strong."

"Yes."

The conversation faltered into silence. They were men; they knew no more.

"He's asked me to be his secretary," said Thomas, throwing a log into the fire.

His father nodded, considerately, and then laughed. "Well, it's better than driving pigs here, there and everywhere for him."

"What do you think I should do?"

"The old man was someone to be reckoned with, you know," said his father, answering the question by way of indulging his own nostalgia. "Figure in the court, you know, in the thick of things. The old Queen had a soft spot for him. Took me with him to London; by God, he was tyrant, too, you wouldn't cross him. Sorry when he died though, but I'd had enough by then, just wanted to get back here."

He paused and spat into the fire.

"Don't know about the son. Lacklustre, I thought, in comparison. Had it too easy. Married a pretty girl though, daughter of Tom Wilford, big family in Kent. Spirited, skittish, I'd say. You see, she thought she'd be entertaining the king, holding her own court in Wales, that's what she imagined, before he died, Prince Henry that is. That took the wind out of her sails. Then, of course, she started to breed, and that's enough to take the wind out of any woman's sails."

"I'll give it a trial," said Thomas, comparing his own picture of the domestic situation at Baron Hill with that of his father's account. "At least until after Sarah's brought to bed. Then I'll take stock."

"If you're thinking of Aberlleiniog," said his father, at last, after they had both stared into the fire for some time, "take the farm down at Lleiniog, that would make a decent house, big enough for a family. By the coast. You could run ships from there. And then you can have the castle as your plaything!"

"I'll give it some thought," said Thomas, with a laugh, acknowledging, even in his father's satire, some sound common sense.

In the bedchamber, Sarah was restless, and there could be no warmth between them. Eventually, as the morning approached, she found some sleep, but Thomas Cheadle found none. As the first birds began to sing, his thoughts turned, in a misty veil of wakefulness, to Lady Anne Bulkeley, of Baron Hill.

Chapter 8

Jenna Shaw was not at all, now, like the zany girl with outrageously spiky blond hair, decorator's bib-and-braces and rainbow striped scarf, who had strutted her stuff across the studio set of *Switch* for four years during the nineties.

She had lived, for two years, in a small terraced house not far from the station in Blackheath. For a long time before that, she had resisted the temptation of property ownership, though people told her that it was the best form of investment, especially with the property boom. Then she had toyed with the idea of taking on a project. She had even had a conversation with Sarah Beeney in a coffee lounge at the BBC when she had promised her a spot on the Property Ladder - then one of the hottest formats on TV - if she went ahead with something that needed doing up, but it was just at that stage that she had got *Country Retreats*, and so the project was dropped, and instead, with a regular salary again, she had taken out a mortgage on the neat little town house that was now her pride and joy.

She loved the village of Blackheath, with its trendy bistros and boutiques, and she loved the walk across the heath itself to Greenwich Park, especially on windy Sundays when the kite fliers were out, and, of course, the station was very convenient for town. Occasionally she went to the Blackheath Halls for a concert, or to a restaurant if a friend stayed, but her main recreation now was collecting furniture, and rugs, and lamps and pictures for the house.

Like a lot of television people she didn't watch much television, preferring to listen to Radio 4 and Radio 3, sometimes Classic FM, though the long commercial breaks irritated her. The music which had accompanied her own rites of passage had been, aged ten, Madonna and Michael Jackson, aged seventeen, Nirvana and Alice in Chains, aged twenty, the Red Hot Chilli Peppers and Nanci Griffith, and occasionally, when friends were round, she put on the old CDs, but that was with the nostalgia of being in her thirties, and her real love was classical music. She adored Mahler, worshipped Bach, and was becoming a committed aficionado of Italian opera.

Her mum, still living in the family home in Reading, had more or less accepted that she was gay, that it wasn't just a phase or a protest, or a quest for individuality. Her brother, on the other hand, still tended to regard it as an affront. It was something he had to confess to his fiancée, as if it was a genetic defect in the family. He was now living in France with Gaynor and his two boys, working from home through the wonders of computer networking, and so awkward social encounters were less frequent.

Her mother now confined herself to a handful of predictable questions: *what about children, dear, don't you want to have children?* Though there was the old favourite: *have you met anyone, yet?* - slipped in as if there was still a racing chance that she might meet someone sufficiently charming and rich to turn her head for long enough to get married and have kids.

"Look mum I just can't do something that's not in my nature."

"Couldn't you just put up with it? Lots of women do. If it's just sex."

"It isn't just sex."

"Your father and I hardly ever had sex at all after Stephen was born."

"Mother!" she called, using the formal term to signify disapproval, "I don't want to know this!"

"Well, I don't know what the fuss is. You don't miss it when you get used to it. It's a blessed relief. As far as I was concerned it had served its purpose."

"And did dad agree with that?"

"He never complained."

Jenna sometimes wondered if her father had had a secret life of promiscuity when he was off globetrotting for the company. Her father remained a mysterious figure – a topic for endless speculation. It's only when someone dies suddenly that you realise how little you know them; at the point when the door has been slammed shut and you realise you can know no more, only then do you understand how much you have taken for granted.

How, she sometimes wondered, would he have reacted to her coming out? Or, more to the point perhaps, would his presence and influence have put pressure on her to stay in the closet? *You wouldn't have decided to be a lesbian if your father was still alive* – she could hear her mother thinking it even though she had never said it.

And what on earth would her father, who read the Daily Telegraph, and who still thought of television as a diluter of culture, have thought of *Switch*?

Of course, now, at the age of thirty-one, she was not at all like the zany girl with outrageously spiky blond hair, decorator's overalls and rainbow striped scarf, who had strutted her stuff across the set of *Switch*.

But then, she never really had been.

Chapter 9

29th September 1831

This morning Isobel and I sketched and painted, for two hours, the view from the terrace which looks across the lawns towards the Menai Strait with the Welsh mountains behind. It was a warm September morning, very still, and quite pleasant enough to be comfortable sitting outside. For me, the main pleasure was seeing Isobel quite herself again, so tranquil and so concentrated for so long a period. The strangest thing, however, was when I looked at the composition of her sketch.

In my own, I had attempted to capture the contours and shadows of the mountains, deeply etched and as clear as crystal. In the foreground I had done little more than a wash of green, and the towers of the castle, hastily sketched in with light pencil lines. Isobel, on the other hand, had concentrated almost entirely on the immediate view, but instead of the close-cut lawns, she had depicted a rough meadow of clover and wild grass, and strangest of all, a woman and two girls who had gathered armfuls of wild flowers.

"You've painted from imagination," I ventured to say.

I saw from the puzzled look on her face that she had misheard or misunderstood.

"The woman and the girls," I explained.

She furrowed her brow.

"Did you imagine them or was it from memory?"

"But they were there," she said. "You saw them, surely!"

I think she could tell, from my look, my misgivings.

"But they walked by, an hour ago," she said. "You must have been so intent on your mountains that you missed them."

"What about the meadow?" I asked.

"What about it?"

"Grass and flowers, don't you see the difference?"

"Oh yes," she said, matter-of-factly, as we packed away our easels.

Later, seeking reassurance, I asked Mrs Thomas if she recognised any such people from her knowledge of the local folk.

"A woman and two little girls," I explained, and showed her Isobel's sketch.

"Bless you, miss," she said, "I don't think I'd recognise anyone in those clothes."

It was an aspect of Isobel's composition which, in my anxiety, I had failed to notice, or which I had simply taken to be a fashion peculiar to the area. The details of the costume were only lightly sketched in, but both the woman and the girls were wearing reticella lace winged collars and starched white caps entirely different in style to anything that might be seen in our modern fashion.

I worried myself for some time, wondering whether or not I should question Isobel further over this, and in the end decided against it. It could do no good. Possibly the opposite. As long as she remains tranquil I am inclined to indulge her other eccentricities.

30th September 1831

We were told a tale, last evening, of an incident which occurred close by here during August of this year, just a few weeks before our own arrival. It has become common, apparently, in the summer months, for pleasure craft to travel to Beaumaris from various places along the coast to the north. One such vessel, the Rothsay Castle, set out from the port of Liverpool on the 17$^{th\ of}$ August on a voyage destined to end in tragedy. The ship itself, if rumour is to be believed, was hardly seaworthy to begin with, and met with high winds and stormy seas off Point of Ayr and the Flintshire coast, a situation not helped by her crew being an ill-sorted body of inept recruits, and her master, by the critical stages of the journey, much the worse in his judgement through the effects of liquor.

Arriving in the waters just off the coast near here in darkness, much later than planned, and still in storm conditions, there was great distress on board, with a company of ninety men women and children now in peril of their lives. By this stage the ship was so disabled as to be incapable of steering a course and she drifted towards a sandbank called the Dutchman's bank which emerges, at low tide, between Beaumaris and Puffin Island. Improvidently prepared as she was, there was no means of attracting attention from the shore, by which means her plight might have been helped. She was driven onto the bank again and again and with each impact poor souls were hurtled overboard to their death. This went on until dawn, when, with the first light, the alarm was raised and a rescue attempt began. Only twenty-three of the crew and company survived, and the bodies of the dead were washed up on the island and on the mainland during the ensuing days. Sir Richard, who was then in residence, deeply moved by the sad occurrence, made money available for the burial of the dead, and sent workers from the estate about the macabre business of discovering bodies washed up.

All this just a few weeks before our arrival! Had we known it at the time, how much more unsettling would have been our own journey across the Lavan Sands, where we must have passed within half a mile of where that doomed ship foundered!

Chapter 10

1623

Spring became summer, and the trees which formed a wide arc around the house on Baron Hill thickened with luxuriant greenery. In June, Thomas Cheadle took up his duties as Sir Richard's secretary, and agent of the Baron Hill Estates.

"You'll need to speak to my agent," said Sir Richard – pleased with this style of address, which he had thought of himself – as he spoke to the Master of Customs, with regard to certain matters of shipping from the port.

"Be sure to acquaint my agent with the details," he said to the Land Registrar, in respect of some farms in Caernarvon which he had recently purchased.

Thomas Cheadle, driven by his own determination, became a figure to be reckoned with by those who were in the business of land and commerce about the island, and he was known to have a shrewd head for legal and financial detail. Titles, deeds, squabbles over land and rent, all manner of lawsuits – he knew how to form alliances with those who had influence in the courts, how to put people in his debt, so that favours might be later called in. His office was established in the library at Baron Hill, and he had accommodation in a private wing of the house, as well as the house in the town, which he kept on.

Towards his employer, Sir Richard Bulkeley, he found himself developing something of an ambivalent attitude. With his air of refinement and breeding, his casual patrician assumptions, he was, in many respects, an impressive figure. He had an easy manner and a natural confidence that disarmed people, but Cheadle sometimes wondered if it were the title and the trappings people deferred to rather than the man. When you looked beneath the façade, there was nothing so special about him; nothing that made him a finer man or a more able man, other than that he had been bred in titled affluence and took superiority to be his natural condition.

"Listen Thomas," he said, one day, "there's a matter I'd like you to deal with for me. A little awkward really. Well, let me explain, judge for yourself. You see, there's a woman, of my acquaintance, as you might say, in Twickenham, recently brought to bed of a son, and damn me if she isn't claiming that the child is mine. Well, of course I have no way of knowing for sure whether I'm the child's father or not, though I have to admit to my shame that I couldn't deny it outright, if you understand me, but anyway, I'd like to do the decent thing, as far as I can, and that's where I require your good offices. Straightforward business, really, set up some arrangement, the mother will be happy enough so long as she's provided for, and I wouldn't want the child brought up a beggar. Set up something for me, will you? I'll let you have the information you need. Then everyone's happy."

"I take it her Ladyship doesn't know of this."

"No. Not a word, mind you. Not a word. Keep things simple, Thomas, always best. Keep things simple."

He visited a solicitor in Chester and set up a trust for the mother and child in Twickenham, to be administered from London. It was the first, but not the only time his master employed him in this office.

At about the same time, an investment which he had recommended to Sir Richard, and one in which he had invested money of his own - a shipping venture to New England - proved successful, and this not only consolidated his position, but also helped to establish the foundation of his own fortune.

Before the autumn, when Sir Richard once more left for London, there was hardly an aspect of the estate's business with which the capable Thomas Cheadle could not be trusted.

In August, he had word from Cheadle that his wife, Sarah, had died giving birth to a son.

Chapter 11

It was then that he should have gone to the colonies.

"Deepest commiserations, Thomas."

"Thank you, Sir Richard."

"All things must come to pass. The will of God. We're in his hands."

"Yes."

"Anyway, time heals. Time heals. What will you do?"

"I haven't decided yet."

"No, well, early days. Of course, if you think this is the right time to go and look for new opportunities…"

"I haven't really had time to think… I once thought to have taken myself to the New World."

"The New World. Well, no-one would blame you. Let me know what you decide."

"What of the child?" said Lady Anne.

"A boy."

"In health?"

"Yes, in health."

"Then, his mother's suffering was not in vain."

"No."

"What will you do with him?"

"He will be brought up in Cheshire. Under my father's roof. His education will be at my father's hand. After that, I know not yet."

"And his name"

"Richard."

She put her hand over his.

"You will stay here, won't you?"

"Madam?"

"My husband says he fears you will leave for the Americas."

"I have considered it."

"Don't go away, Thomas," she said, her hand still resting lightly on his, her voice as soft as muslin close to his ear. "Stay, for my sake."

Thomas Cheadle made no reply. But his veins hatched red with desire.

Chapter 12

Switch! How had it all come about?

Her last year at university. Finals approaching. It was all coming to an end. The real world beckoning with an uncompromising finger.

She listed all the serious careers: civil servant, teacher, accountant, journalist, something in publishing, or local government?

Nothing, at that stage, really did it.

"I'd just like to do something a bit mad first," she said to her friends.

Backpack around the world? Do voluntary service? White-water rapids in Venezuela?

She went to an audition at a hotel in Earls Court for a new children's TV show [no name at that stage] for Silver Lining, a small independent production company.

There were seventy girls auditioning for the single female role, most of them just out of – or still in – stage school, and because she regarded her chances as being absolutely zero, she had felt no nerves or inhibitions at all, doing little improvisational things they asked for that she hadn't the slightest idea she could do.

They called her back two weeks later, on her own– though she fully supposed other girls had made it to this stage too – and now there was a camera to perform to. This time she didn't think it went particularly well, and was desperately disappointed, but a further call-back, the following week was organised in a group of three – herself and two boys, and this seemed to go well – there was a good chemistry between them the producer said [didn't they say that to everyone?]

What she didn't realise [what none of them realised it turned out later] was that this was the first meeting of the *Switch* team.

It was intended for a younger audience at first, but for some reason, according to audience research, the pilots were ticking more boxes with teenagers, and so the format was tweaked slightly, the content was made a bit more sparky, and it went out in a three-hour slot on Saturday morning.

There were regular features, team contests, silly games, lots and lots of coloured paints. Then, guests from the pop world – *Lads To Go*, *Boy Frenz*, *Wanda Rockheart*, live performances, phone-ins, the whole merry-go-round of studio fun and action.

In those pre-digital days of four terrestrial channels when the use of the internet for kids' leisure was in its infancy, the show quickly developed a loyal fan base.

There were three of them: Switch, Swivel and Swatch. She was Swatch.

Switch – Dave Ryder – was, everyone agreed, the promising one, the most popular, the charismatic one – the one for whom a bright future was promised. When the show was over, he tried, unsuccessfully for a pop career, and then disappeared. Now, according to Jenny Lester, who had been his girlfriend at one point, he was working as a social worker in Peckham.

Ian Rawles – Swivel – was the geeky one, dozy, bespectacled, inept. He went on to play small parts in a season in Stratford, notably Flute in *A Midsummer Night's Dream*, then landed a role in an American backed film with an American leading lady, Lucy Pettifer playing an English socialite, and was now in Hollywood, on call to play certain recognisable English character types, and making, so it was said, an absolute packet.

Jenna went a year without work after *Switch*, then got some TV commercial voice-over work, which paid the bills, and then, out of the blue, along came *Country Retreats*. Quentin Sykes, the main presenter during the twelve years the programme had been airing, was retiring and they had decided on a shake-up, keeping the name – a by-word for solid broadcasting values and also something very English – but revamping the format and bringing in new presenters.

She jumped at the chance.

Every week she had a project – rural communities, their trials, tribulations, customs, their little triumphs, their pubs, their post-offices, their Am-Dram etc. The occasional incidental references to *Switch* [to be fair there weren't many] by locals who recognised and remembered, were discreetly edited out.

It was a team of five. Callum Jefferson, the main presenter and front-man, Tom Sykes who looked at the local property market wherever they were located, James Rothwell took on local commerce and industry, and Jenny Lewis the biologist and horticulturalist, who provided a scientific angle.

The programme had a small but reliable audience, and in the search for relatively inexpensive content for the digital age it was a banker.

And for Jenna it provided an important stepping-stone from the ephemera of kids' TV to more substantial broadcasting. What the next step would be [hoping there was one] she didn't really know, but, as Bex, her agent had said, an appearance on *What's My Lineage* certainly wouldn't do her CV any harm.

She poured a glass of wine, put on the CD Rolando Villazon, Italian Operatic Arias, which she had bought up in town that morning, and thought about Maisie Flood.

It was not always possible to be sure, of course. She had once made a disastrous misjudgement at a party in Sevenoaks which had nearly ruined an entire weekend, but usually she could tell. With some people it was blatantly obvious, of course, but more often it was an intuition, a sixth sense, an intriguing moment of tuning into someone else's thoughts and the equal intrigue of wondering if she was tuning into yours.

It was ten days now since the meeting at Lavender Street. She had spoken to her mother three or four times in the interim, and her initial horror at the thought of being on camera, had mellowed into something which now sounded distinctly like enthusiasm.

"I haven't spoken to Stephen," she said, "well, you know what he's like about anything public, but I expect he'll be all right when he gets used to it."

"How can he get used to it if you haven't told him?"

"Oh, I'll tell him afterwards," she said, archly.

A couple of researchers had been round, she told Jenna. "They were very nice," she added, and then, with a typical non-sequitur, "I'd just baked some of my scones."

Jenna could picture the scene: scones, clotted cream, jam, tea, the best China service. They would not have escaped the treatment.

"Oh, and someone called Maisie Flood telephoned..."

Jenna's ears pricked up.

"You know how bad I am with names, but I remembered her because isn't there a poem where a mazy flood is a winding river, I'm sure there is somewhere, Milton or somebody, anyway, she telephoned, and then said she'd be in touch with you. Do you know her?"

"Oh, just vaguely," said Jenna.

"Well, anyway, she sounded very nice," she concluded, with her characteristic seal of approval.

Winding river, thought Jenna, caught in a moment of abstraction after she had put down the telephone, *what a lovely idea!*

Chapter 13

Beaumaris, 30th September 1831.

My dearest James,

It may be madness of me to attempt this letter, even greater madness to think that I might find some means of ensuring that it reaches you, but as it is madness that both my guardian and my sister would assert to be my true condition, and as I sometimes stand in considerable doubt of my own sanity, I will attempt it, nevertheless.

What a dreadful sequence of events followed our last meeting! Having forced me to return to Evesham Place, Mr Harcourt kept me watched in the house for two days, and so strenuous were my protests that at last Dr Fairhurst was persuaded to administer a sedative, for fear, as he explained it, that I would decline into a hysterical fit and thence into a delirious fever. I cannot explain the nightmare forms and lugubrious visions which beset me in the ensuing days, nor can I remember how one day was distinguished from another, for all merged together in a terrible twilight world in which I existed. I am told by my sister that this period lasted for ten days, and that for some part of that time, she was in fear of my life; indeed, I believe that without her tender ministrations I should not have survived. For some time following this, I remained in a condition of extreme weakness, able only to take three tablespoons of broth for sustenance before the sickness returned, and more often than not in a mental state of such debility that my own thoughts scarcely seemed to belong to me.

During the first stages of my convalescence, I was allowed only short walks around the square, which has some pleasant trees providing shade from the summer sun – for it was by now already

July – and all my thoughts were of you, though they were flimsy almost ethereal thoughts, as much of a ghost or spirit encountered in a dream as of a living person. Later, accompanied by my sister and guardian, I was permitted to go in the chaise as far as Kensington Gardens and the Serpentine, and I gazed through the trees and through the passing crowds in the sad hope of catching a glimpse of your face, but in vain.

It was decided eventually, as my strength returned, that, for the better recovery of my health, I should quit London altogether, and to that end Sir Richard Bulkeley made the offer of Baron Hill, his country seat in Wales, as a place suitable for that purpose.

Of the five-day journey from London, I remember almost nothing until we came to Conway in North Wales, and I must tell you of something that happened there which caused me considerable disquiet. We arrived just before noon and after taking some refreshment, we walked near the harbour, which is very busy with fishing boats and other small craft and affords a splendid view towards the magnificent suspension bridge and the imposing, though somewhat menacing, castle which dominates the town.

There was a fresh sea breeze which had a wonderful restorative effect on me, and for the first time in many weeks, I felt clear in my thoughts and full of spirit. Emily tried to persuade me to return to our lodgings for a rest in the late afternoon, but I refused and insisted instead that we be allowed to visit the castle.

The starkness of the steep castle walls viewed from outside is matched by the bleak and desolate aspect within. But there is something noble and sublime in such ancient places which awakens the romantic spirit of which you and I used to speak so often. Indeed, I was caught in a very pleasant reverie of imagining you coming here to paint the scene, with me, of course, your dearest of companions, when I felt such an icy chill passing through my body that I all but fainted. Emily, who had walked on, ran back to support me, but my head was spinning wildly, and I seemed to hear sniggering and mocking laughter, and I heard myself crying Stop them! Stop them! repeatedly though I knew not what it was that so provoked me to call out.

When I was at last sufficiently recovered we returned to our lodging and a doctor was summoned, but he could find no cause – so diminished by this time were my symptoms – other than the rigours of travel, though he added that people were sometimes known to be adversely affected by the melancholy nature of such surroundings. He prescribed rest and administered a mild sleeping draft to that purpose.

Throughout the night I was visited by wakeful intermissions in which the most oppressive though indeterminate images troubled my thoughts. Time and time again I felt that some terrible act was being perpetrated that I must try to stop though I was powerless to do so.

The following day, I woke late, and as a result the final stage of our journey to Anglesey was delayed. We were persuaded by Mr Hughes, our guide, to cross the strait using the old ferry, and it was here, for no apparent reason at all that I again felt that chill passing along my spine with an apprehension of some terrible horror, but thankfully it passed quickly and on our arrival I spent a night of peaceful slumber.

Hence it is, after a journey of some five days, that I now write to you from Beaumaris, where, with only dear Emily to watch over me, I am able, for the first time in all these months, to find such privacy as is required for this purpose.

Oh, my dear James, why, oh why did you delay our departure from Dartford on that fateful morning? Would we not otherwise have been beyond my guardian's reach that very day, and by now – it squeezes my heart with both pleasure and pain to think of it – I would have been your wife! Was it some scruple of doubt on your part, my dear James? Did you question your love for me in that moment?

But I torment myself with this question only to confirm to myself that I do not believe it! The sincerity of your vows I did not doubt then and I do not doubt them now. I fully believe that your wishes were as mine, and that you were as fully committed as I to a life together, and it is this that has sustained me through all this turbulent period of my illness, like a stream running unseen beneath the rugged surface next to the very bedrock.

I am certain that one day, this long interim of separation,

however painful now, will seem as nothing, merely a test of our constancy and resolution, and I comfort myself with the thought that your feelings are as one with mine.

Oh, my dear James, I am filled with sudden dread that this letter will not find you, and that you will conclude at last from my silence that my heart has grown cold. Please, please write to me by return of post to rid me of this fear. Even the briefest of notes will suffice to make my heart soar.

In the meantime, I will try to wing my thoughts to you through the air, so that you will know that I prize your love more than life itself, and that I would gladly sacrifice all that I hold most dear to be by your side, and give myself to you body and soul.

I am your most devoted friend and servant [I would say wife]

Isobel Harcourt.

Chapter 14

1625

It was a poor summer of withering winds and almost constant rain; across the island crops rotted in the field, and not for the first time, the people steeled themselves for a winter of hunger.

At Beaumaris, in August, there was an outbreak of typhus, and this prompted Sir Richard to bring forward the date of his return to London. Lady Anne and her daughters, it was decided, would accompany him, along with the son, Richard, who was returning to Lincoln's Inn.

"I'm closing the main part of the house," said Sir Richard, rather wearily. "Have them drape the furniture, and so on, but see they keep it aired, will you, Thomas, don't want to invite the mildew. Keep the library open for yourself, of course. There are some papers from Gronant I want you to look at, something about tenancies, you'll be able to sort it out, no doubt. You can write to me in London if there are any problems."

He went to stand by the window, watching the rain streaming down the panes.

"Filthy day," he said. "Filthy place, when it's like this, don't you think?"

"I'm sure London will be a welcome change."

He shrugged, giving out an air of profound world weariness. He was not pleased, Cheadle surmised, that the entire family was to accompany him. He was used to going to London alone. It was his playground.

He doesn't appreciate what he's got, Cheadle found himself thinking, he doesn't know how to value things. It was his father who made all the achievements – he just lives on them like a well-bred parasite.

"I wondered if I might ask," Cheadle began, having decided to brooch the matter before Sir Richard's departure, "about Aberlleiniog."

"Oh, yes, what about it?"

He outlined his plan for restoring the site, putting buildings there, perhaps adding an outpost to the island's defences. He expected Sir Richard to be curious, amused, sceptical, but in fact he showed every sign of being interested in the project not in the least.

"Of course," Cheadle concluded, his own enthusiasm beginning to wane in the face of his master's indifference, "the ground would need to be cleared first, and the road opened up."

"And who," said Sir Richard, with sudden imperious disdain, "is to pay for this? Is it proposed that I am to underwrite this venture of yours? Am I to pay for this?"

"It would be my intention," said Cheadle, suppressing a sudden intense dislike for the supercilious posturing, "to finance the project myself."

"Oh, well, do as you like," he said, with a languid wave of his hand. "Do as you like, draw up a lease, The place is of no interest to me. None whatsoever."

The following day, Cheadle accompanied them to the ferry. The sky had lifted a little, and it was dry, but there was a chill wind from the north east. The girls, Ann and Mary were excited about the journey, and playful, but the boy was sullen and resentful, not wanting to exchange the freedom of his vacation for the disciplines of school. Sir Richard was irritable, with occasional outbursts of petulant ill-temper. Lady Anne was self-preoccupied, uncommunicative. Cheadle tried to catch a glimpse of her eye, to exchange a look, to read a sign, perhaps, but she avoided his glance.

Riding away, he felt angry, badly used, but then chastised himself. He had no right to expect anything from her. Usually, after Sir Richard's departure, there was a pleasant easy mood about the house, a sense of complacency, with just a hint of dalliance between them. But it was frivolous to think it had any meaning, after all.

Now, however, he reflected, was the time to consider leaving, making a new future elsewhere.

He rode out to Aberlleiniog, where only the weeds and the extravagant undergrowth had prospered since his last visit; the sound of the horse's hoofs was muffled by the fullness of the surrounding vegetation, and the ground was sodden with weeks of rain. Droplets of rain clung to the spiders' webs stretched between fronds of bracken, and the last of the meadow-sweet was giving of a faint odour, slightly rotten, like privet, the smell of earth, the smell of death.

He turned away and began to ride back towards Beaumaris. It would be, after all, a misbegotten venture, he concluded, a fool's errand.

Business took him to Chester, two days later, and he continued his journey to Cheshire, where his son, Richard, was now a year old, crawling and walking and climbing everywhere with boundless energy like a curious and fearless puppy, and with his grandfather always at his tail to catch him when he fell.

"I've been thinking," he said to his father, when the child was at last asleep, "maybe the time has come for me to make a change, start off elsewhere."

His father looked up sharply. "Why? You've prospered well enough there, haven't you?"

"Well enough, perhaps, but it's not the only place on the earth."

"Better the devil you know."

"You've changed your tack, haven't you?"

The old man shrugged his shoulders. Thomas Cheadle realised his fear was of the child being taken from them. He didn't raise the subject again.

In the second week of September, the skies over Anglesey cleared, and the warmth of June returned, so that it might have been an island in a southern sea. On a sudden impulse, Thomas

Cheadle hired a dozen labourers from the town and took them out to Aberlleiniog in a wagon with scythes and saws and axes, instructing them to clear away the growth from the mound itself and around the outer ditch.

"What whim is this?" came the voice of a man, emerging on horseback from the trees, with a boy on the saddle in front of him. It was Sir Thomas Bulkeley, Sir Richard's younger brother, and his son, who had been given the traditional Bulkeley Christian name of the eldest son. "Has my brother taken leave of his senses?"

"What is it, father?" said the child.

The father lowered him to the ground. He was a well-set lad of seven or eight, and he immediately took hold of a scythe and tried to use it, much to the amusement of those around.

"Take care you don't cut your own legs off," said his father. "Then your mother would have to cut your new breeches down."

The child held the scythe towards him like a weapon, threatening, causing further laughter.

"It's my own project," Cheadle explained.

Sir Thomas nodded, looked around, weighing it up. "Yes, I might have known my brother wouldn't think of something like this."

He had something of the same self-assurance as Sir Richard, but he was more forthright, with a little less of the veneer of cultivated manners. He lived at Hen Plas, the family home in Beaumaris before the father built Baron Hill. Thomas Cheadle disliked him but respected him more than his elder brother.

"They knew what they were doing when they picked this spot," he said. "Whoever they were. What are you going to do with it?"

"Get it cleared. See how it looks. Build something perhaps."

"A fortification?"

"Perhaps."

"Set a garrison here and you could defend it against the rest of Anglesey."

"I wasn't considering that."

Sir Thomas laughed. "Come on, boy," he called, and the lad jumped up and allowed himself to be pulled onto the saddle.

"When will I have my own horse?" he asked, as they rode off.

"Soon enough," his father replied.

After five days, the rampart was cleared of the main surface vegetation, and a bonfire was lit to burn it off; then they drew the fire over the surrounding turf to scorch it and destroy some of the roots. Thomas Cheadle began to plan the logistics of bringing stone around the coast from the quarries of Llandona and Bychan.

When he returned to his quarters at Baron Hill that night, word had come with the post from London that Lady Anne Bulkeley was to return to Beaumaris before the end of the month.

Chapter 15

"Hi Jenna. Maisie here. Sorry about the delay. Anyway, we've fixed up for next Tuesday, if that's OK with you. Will that be OK with your mum, do you think?"

"I'll give her a call, but she's on standby. All agog. Wetting herself with excitement and trepidation! Probably been hoovering up and doing the garden for two weeks in anticipation."

"Right, well, we've got you a first-class ticket, and Jonty Fox will come with you. Jonty's the cameraman, by the way. We'll get some footage of you travelling up there, speeding along sort of thing, looking very thoughtful, and then we'll put a bit of voiceover on that afterwards. I'll meet you there. I'm travelling up with Simon in the van, so that we can get the lights and sound set up, and so I can case the joint, of course. Does that sound OK?"

"Fine."

"So, you can start your journey now!"

"Tell me, Maisie, do you know what my story is, I mean, do you tell me where we're going with this journey?"

"Well, not everything. And there are usually some unexpected outcomes, too. But it's nice if we can get you to look, you know, quite surprised at times."

"OK. I'll do my best!"

Chapter 16

2nd October 1831

I am growing concerned that my sister Isobel is far from cured of her infatuation with James Pennington. This morning, in the village, whilst I was in the haberdasher's waiting to be served, she excused herself, saying that she wanted to order some oil pastels from the stationer's. When I came out onto the street, a few minutes later, having, through my misgivings – now second nature to me I'm afraid where Isobel is concerned – foreshortened my business at the haberdasher's, I saw her coming from the opposite direction along Castle Street, having just emerged from a side street where the post office is located. There were just sufficient people on the main street to prevent her from seeing me and I stepped into the baker's shop and joined the queue there for long enough to let her pass by. I then quickly made my way to the post office.

"Excuse me," I said to the post mistress, a tiny bespectacled lady who, like many of the shopkeepers, thank goodness, speaks perfectly good English as well as Welsh. "I'm looking for my sister. I don't suppose a young lady in a pale blue cape and bonnet has been in here in the last few minutes."

"Why, yes, she left just a short time ago."

"Oh good. I'm so relieved. She must have remembered the letter to her guardian, at last!"

"Her guardian."

"Yes. Mr Pennington."

Here I was ashamed of my own subterfuge, but it produced the desired effect.

"Well, then, you can rest assured. That was certainly the name on the envelope she left."

"Thank you so much. We're staying at the house on Baron Hill. We're sure to be coming in here quite often."

"I'll look forward to that, miss."

I returned her smile and turned towards the door; then, turning back with another smile, I added, "oh, please, if you don't mind, don't say anything about this to my sister when she comes in here again. She is very forgetful, but she'd be mortified if she thought I was keeping watch over her."

I hurriedly made my way back to Castle Street and stepped into the little bookshop on the corner. Five minutes later, Isobel appeared, with her pastels.

I had already decided to say nothing directly to her. I could gain nothing from it, and could possibly lose her trust, which would be the worst possible outcome. I simply made my mind up to keep up the pretence – as I always do – that everything is normal, and in the meantime I sought the first opportunity to pen a hasty note to Mr Harcourt, asking for his advice. The post mistress was pleased to see me again, and she reassured me that my letter would go, overnight, with the same post as Isobel's.

Chapter 17

1625

For days they had been lighting fires across the island, burning off what was left of the stubble and the rotten crops, trying to burn out the disease from the earth. From every vantage point, columns of smoke could be seen, snaking upwards and mixing in the hazy air above. The leaves on the trees had turned a fiery red. It was the third week in October.

That morning, a cargo of stone from Red Wharf had been landed at Traeth Penmon, and the groundwork at Aberlleiniog was making steady progress, with foundations dug on three sides where the outer walls would be built. All day, mule drawn carts had been ferrying the stone from the shore to the site.

It was in the anticipation of Lady Anne's return that Thomas Cheadle had taken the decision to move his project through to its next stage. In spite of himself, he could not disguise the lightness of excitement he felt at the prospect of seeing her again, and he had wanted to fill the time with something as ambitious and unlikely as his Aberlleiniog scheme.

"I'd like to see it. Will you take me there?" she asked when he told her of the progress that had been made.

The preparations for her return had been hastily carried out, fires lit in all the rooms, the shutters and windows opened during the day to clear the damp air, the kitchen restocked, maids working to polish the furniture and the woodwork, the bedrooms re-made and aired.

There was nothing to report of her time in London, or if there was, she said little. The boy was not a good scholar; she doubted his ability to persevere with a legal education. The girls were staying with their aunt for a further two weeks; she did not want to bring them back until she was absolutely certain that the typhus had gone: did he have any news of that?

"In London," she said, "they call it the prison fever, for that is where the lice breed most freely, where it is overcrowded, and the lice carry it from one person to the next, they say."

On the day after her return, they had dined together, and though they had spoken of nothing other than the business of the household and the estate, and related matters, there was a curious mixture of tension and pleasure being in each other's company with no others present. It was usually the girls, with their constant chatter and laughter, who set the tone of their meetings.

It was then that he had first mentioned Aberlleiniog to her.

"Sir Richard didn't mention the conversation I had with him about the scheme?"

"No," she said with studied neutrality. It was impossible to read any meaning from her reply and yet there seemed to be a world of meaning behind it.

It was on the day of the bonfires that he took her there, in the open wagon.

"Where will the house be?" she asked.

"Where we're standing now."

He moved away, pacing the distance, and then indicated where the outer corner would be, describing the outline of the building with his arms.

"How long will it take?"

"Two years, three years. Maybe less. These masons shake their heads and whistle. They always want you to appreciate the full extent of the problem before they'll admit they can solve it. That's their professional code."

They made their way back to where they had left the wagon, and Cheadle took the reins. The light was fading now, and the workmen had already gone, taking their tools. In the trees, the cawing of rooks, and the occasional sound of wings, breaking twigs, could be heard. When they reached the top of the hill, the light of the bonfires could be seen, now bright with the onset of darkness, spreading below, and the sharp smell of smoke mingled with the rich odour of autumnal decay.

He pulled back on the reins to stop the horse so that they could watch. Then he slipped his hand over hers, and in reply she opened her hand, allowing their palms to touch, and their fingers to intermingle, exchanging a world of meaning.

"Let me come to you, for God's sake," he said. "This has been going on for long enough."

"We put ourselves in such great peril," she murmured.

"Yes."

"The dangers are greater for a woman than a man."

He knew this was true.

"We must be seen less in each other's company or people will talk."

"Is that all?"

"Thomas, I have to know that I can trust you."

"What proof do you need?"

There was a long silence; only the twittering of swallows in the dwindling light.

"Come to me, then," she said at last. "But on the third or fourth day before the new moon. Not before that, or later."

He tilted his head in a question.

"I have only ever conceived in the third quarter of the moon. That is my time."

He nodded his understanding: there must be no child.

"Come to the room along the corridor from the second staircase."

"The nursery?"

"They call it the nursery but it has never been one. I sleep there sometimes. My maid won't think it amiss. It shares a door with my chamber."

Anticipation, Thomas Cheadle discovered, is a powerful aphrodisiac. No love potion could have worked a stronger effect on him than the recollection of Lady Anne Bulkeley's words, as five days elapsed to the time she had appointed; and no fear could be more jealously tantalising than the fear that some chance incident would interpose to prevent their appointed meeting.

But at last the day arrived, and at last the daylight lingered, and at last the household was at rest and the house was in silence. He made his way through the shadows of the hall to the point on the staircase where the second staircase branched off.

The room was in darkness, the air warm and mothy, with a faint hint of meadow-sweet. In the stillness, as his eyes adjusted to the darkness, he heard the quiet click of the lock behind him, and then, turning, felt her fingers touching his face.

Such was the hour that followed, that, in the ensuing weeks, indeed months and years, there could be no remission from restlessness for either of them, but in the uncertain and sometimes anguished anticipation of another such, and yet another such hour again.

Part 2

Chapter 18

London, October 1831

James Pennington was woken from a deep and, at least in part, alcohol induced sleep, by a loud noise downstairs, the rapping of a cane on the door of his lodging. He pulled the blanket over his head for a moment, then pushed it aside, drew on his breeches and boots, and, fastening the buttons of his shirt, made his way down the stairs. He was not so well off that he could afford to lose a commission, if, by some remote chance, that was what it was. By no means!

The cane rapped again.

"All right, all right, damn you!" he called, unfastening the bolts. Then, opening the door, and recognising the visitor, "What do you want?"

"Business, you dog!"

"I have no business with you."

"Hear me out," said the figure, pushing past him, and making his way up the stair.

In the room above, Pennington drew the curtain across the top end of the room to conceal the form of Meg Liddle, asleep in the bed, and turned to face his visitor.

"Is this the only place we can talk?"

"My studio!" said Pennington, with a broad, mocking gesture. "Here's where I do my business."

"Quite so," said the visitor, with a sneer of distaste. "Meet me in the coffee house at the corner of the road in twenty minutes."

"And what if I don't?"

"There's money in it for you."

"You still owe me money."

"The work was never completed. Twenty minutes. Don't keep me waiting."

"What does he want?" asked Meg, when the visitor had gone.

"Never mind my pretty fool!" said Pennington, pulling open the curtain, and sitting on the side of the bed to adjust his boots.

"Come back to bed!" she murmured, pressing up against him. He half turned, kissed her neck and watched his own hand fondling the soft, plump flesh inside her open smock.

Temptation brimmed. Damn him. Let him be damned!

"Not now!" he said at last.

Her face took on a certain expression of haughty disdain; the same expression on the same face was rendered on the canvas on the easel in the middle of the room, so that whatever conclusion the visitor might have drawn from seeing her in Pennington's bed, he might well have also concluded, had he taken the trouble to observe the unfinished portrait, that she was also his model.

Letting himself out, Pennington crossed the road and made his way through the stalls of Jennyfield market to Timothy Black's coffee house. At this time of the morning, just after ten o'clock, it was not busy. Two men at the window tables were reading broadsheets and smoking pipes. The visitor, Roger Harcourt, was sitting in a corner at the far end of the room.

Pennington sat down, waving aside the attentions of Peter, the waiter.

"I'll come to the point, then," said Harcourt. "It may well be the case that you receive letters from my ward."

"And what if I do?"

"There's five guineas for every one you return to me unopened."

"You seem very sure of my capacity for betrayal."

"Oh, I am. I am. I have no doubt of it. And neither do you."

"Ten guineas then if you're so sure of me."

Harcourt let out a contemptuous breath, enough to snuff out a candle.

"What about my work?"

"What work?"

"The work you commissioned."

"You tried to debauch my niece. Your commission is forfeit."

"But now you seek my help."

"Very well. Bring me the portrait so that I may destroy it. Then you shall have your fee. What do you say?"

"Damn you!" said Pennington.

"If I am any judge," said Harcourt, "that does not amount to an outright rejection of my offer."

"Damn you again!"

"Well, you may well wish me damned, but just in case you reach a more mature consideration on either of the two points of business we have discussed, here is my card. I have no doubt that you are familiar with the address already, but if you keep this in your pocket book, it may serve to remind you. Business is business, you know that as well as I, and there are some areas of a man's life where sentiment has no place."

"Damn you again!" said Pennington.

"Good!" said Harcourt. "From that very terse reply, I conclude that we understand each other. Don't ask for me personally, my valet Mobbes is conversant with the matter and is fully empowered to deal with it. That way we may be spared the very unpleasant experience of ever seeing each other again. Or send a messenger, if you like, if you know anyone you would trust with money; but no, perhaps it is unreasonable of me to think that likely. So, do as you please."

"Where is she?" called Pennington, as Harcourt stood and made to go.

Harcourt turned and smiled. "A long way from here. Much further, shall we say, than Dartford!" And then he was gone.

When he returned to his lodging, Meg was still there. She had dressed and was pinning back her hair.

"Am I to sit for you today?" she asked.

"What?"

"Am I to sit for you?"

"I'll do no work today. Go away and come back tomorrow, or

the next day, or the day after that. I don't care."

"He's said something to upset you, hasn't he, that gentleman who called?"

"Upset me? No. He inspired me."

"Inspired you?"

"Yes. To think of a way of murdering him."

"You'd do no such thing."

"Do you think I lack the courage?"

"I think you'd rather not hang."

"Very true. I don't think this neck was made for the hangman's collar. "

"Then…?

"Go away and come back when you feel like it."

"Am I to have anything? For sitting yesterday?"

"You've had your bed and board, haven't you, what more do you want?"

"You should treat me right," Meg protested, used as she was to arguing for everything she got, and to being pushed about, this way and that, before she got it. "You said yourself, I keep the stillest of anybody."

"You do," said Pennington, "you do. So what do you think you're worth?"

"A sixpence, same as usual."

"Here's a shilling, damn it. Come back tomorrow. And don't go being so still for anybody else, mind."

"I shan't," she said gratefully "You can be sure of that."

Chapter 19

Meg Liddle made her way along Jennyfield Lane, then turned into Vinegar Gardens, the start of a fifteen-minute walk which led to her lodgings, a tiny attic room up five staircases over a fishmonger's in Gooseberry Lane. At the bakers on the corner of Vinegar Gardens, she stopped to buy a hot meat pie, and because it was a fine, warm autumn morning, she sat on a wall facing the gardens to eat it, sharing the last crumbs of pastry with the pigeons who had gathered expectantly around her.

Meg Liddle had been brought up, from the age of four, by her grandmother, and she could remember no other parent. Her grandmother had employment in a washhouse close to the river, and because the old woman didn't know what else to do with her, she took the little girl with her to work and bundled her in a corner where she could get up to no mischief. If, when she began to grow up, Meg Liddle developed a particular liking for places that were pleasantly warm, that was probably because she had spent a great deal of her infancy and childhood in places that were unpleasantly cold.

Much of what Meg Liddle had learned about human nature, she had learned from life in the washhouse. There were people there who were peevish, and called her a nuisance, and said that she had no business to be there at all; there were some who were kind and gave her a tit-bit of something if there was anything to give. One old lady, a tiny crippled woman who looked as if she might well have been brought there herself because somebody didn't know what else to do with her, taught her enough of her letters to be able to read. But her abiding memory of the washhouse was that everyone in it, her grandmother included, had arms and hands that were perpetually red and raw from immersion in cold water, and her main childish ambition was to get through her life without having her own arms and hands similarly discoloured.

Away from the washhouse her grandmother had a passing liking for gin, and Meg had been bundled into other corners where she could get up to no mischief, whilst her grandmother indulged this other way of occupying her time. Another strand of Meg's early education had been provided in venues dedicated to this purpose.

The skills with which this education had furnished her, apart from reading and writing, were twofold; firstly, rigorously enforced instruction had given her a high level of aptitude in the art of sitting still, an art which, as she had reminded James Pennington that morning, made her uniquely fitted for her chosen profession of artist's model; secondly, long hours spent sitting still, had provided her with the opportunity of observing other people, their habits and mannerisms of speech, and by the age of eight, she had displayed, for her grandmother's entertainment, and sometimes for the entertainment of others who were to be found in premises where gin was available, an amusing ability to mimic any kind of person she was asked to mimic.

"Do us the drayman, Meg, the one with the lisp…" Meg would oblige.

"Do us the fishwife on the wharf, Meg, the one with the foul mouth…" Meg would oblige.

"Do us a prince of the realm…" and Meg would oblige, using her imagination to turn on the airs and graces of a well-bred gentleman.

Her grandmother was kindly and forgetful and careless; in the main her kindliness prevailed, but she became increasingly forgetful, and eventually she was careless enough to die, leaving Meg, at the age of twelve, alone to look after herself.

The old woman was buried in Lowfield cemetery in a location, which, though now much overgrown, Meg could remember very precisely. And it was from this, as she set about the business of looking after herself, that Meg's morality took its bearings, for the business of looking after herself sometimes entailed doing things which, as she said herself, would make her grandmother turn over in her grave.

She was a warm-hearted girl but she soon learned that warm-heartedness was not a commodity which, on its own, was sufficient for survival; she was hungry for affection, but she soon learned that, like other forms of hunger, it sometimes had to be endured. Looking after herself from the age of twelve to the age of twenty which she now was, had entailed learning, as she said to herself, some tricks of the trade, and she had not achieved it without cultivating some qualities of slyness, mendacity, duplicity, and a host of other venalities, but all of them in reasonable measure, and if she was assumed by many to be a lot worse than she actually was, the truth was that she had probably caused her grandmother far fewer revolutions in that final resting place than she herself often thought to be the case.

Chapter 20

Evesham Place, 2nd October 1831

My dearest Emily,

Your letter has indeed revived my anxieties concerning Isobel's well-being and state of mind. However, I consider your decision to maintain a discreet silence the correct one. If, as seems to be the case, her spirits are so enervated, and her temper and composure so fragile, it is likely that any disclosure of your communication with me will seem a betrayal, which may provoke a further hysterical reaction, and then there is no telling what may be the consequences.

Keep a close watch over her, my dearest Emily, and inform me of any further instances of her wayward behaviour, especially in respect of letters sent from her to London. I will make it my business, as soon as my affairs permit, to join you at Baron Hill so that I may judge at first-hand how we may best proceed in her recuperation. I have already informed Lord Bulkeley of my intention and have his fullest support. In the meantime, I will speak further with Doctor Fairhurst and take his advice.

Your affectionate guardian

Roger Harcourt

Chapter 21

"Right," said Maisie, "so we walk up the garden path and mum comes to the door, quick friendly greeting, then we cut to inside. Cup of tea and cakes which you make a joke about. Then you sit together at the table and mum points out who's who from the photograph album, and you ask some questions, even though you already know some of the answers. We can deal with all that in editing later, for now it's just a case of getting the conversation going along. Is that OK?"

It took three takes to get into the house. During the first, the telephone rang in the hall, a neighbour curious to know what was going on; during the second, a noisy motorbike chose precisely the wrong moment to drive down the road.

"It happens all the time," said Jenna to her mum, who was apologising to Maisie and the cameraman as if it were her fault that things hadn't been better arranged.

"That must be so frustrating!"

"OK, let's try again."

This time it worked, and they proceeded to the photograph albums.

"This, of course," said mum, with mild disapproval, "is your dad."

Jenna managed to suppress a strong urge to laugh but took the photograph from her.

"OK," said Maisie. "Can you just get a close-up of that, Jonty?"

"Are we allowed to stop and start? Can we talk in between?"

"Yes,' said Jenna. 'They'll just edit in all the snippets they need later."

"So they can edit it out if I say something silly."

"Yes, mother."

"Oh, well, that's a relief."

"Or they might keep it in just to make you look really stupid."

"Jenna! That's not a very nice thing to say in front of Maisie."

"OK, let's carry on."

"So, dad came to England in the sixties?"

"Yes. His company opened up a branch in London, and then one in Bristol. That's where we met."

"And where was dad's family from, in America, I mean?"

The details about Jenna's father, Walter Shaw, were sketchy. The family, it seemed, originated in the town of Apple Ridge, Virginia, though he had never lived there, or, so far as mum knew, ever been back there to visit. His own childhood had been in various cities, Los Angeles, Boston, New York as his father travelled around following his own career as a salesman with a company developing synthetics.

"And this," said mum, "is my grandmother, Elsie."

"She looks just like you, mum."

"She does not!!!"

"She does. When you put on a stern face, you'd look like sisters."

"They used to make pickles, I think."

"Pickles?"

"Yes. It was a family business at first, I think, then a factory. In Shrewsbury. They had quite a lot of money at one time, so the story goes. Don't know what happened to all that!"

"So, where do we go from here?" asked Jenna, when the session was over.

"Well," said Maisie. "We may have a lead in America. We're following that up with our sister company, there, they have a branch in Richmond, so we'll see what happens, maybe whisk you off to the states for a few days. Meantime, we're also trying to track down the factory, though from what your mum says, the building itself was probably knocked down between the wars. Anyway, I'll give you a call."

"Right."

"She seems a very nice girl," said mum, when the crew had departed.

"Maisie?"

"Yes. Do you know her?"

"Not really. Just to do with this."

"She's not...one of your friends then," said mum, with a certain inflection.

"No!"

"Well, I can never tell."

"Anyway, none of your business."

Jenna had never brought girlfriends home. Acceptance was one thing; she rather doubted that her mother would be comfortable with that kind of introduction, let alone with her sharing a bed with someone in the family home.

"You haven't met anyone, then?"

"You mean am I about to meet Mr Darcy, get married and have his children?"

"Well, you could do a lot worse."

"The answer's no."

"Such a pity. It's so nice to have little ones about the place."

"You'll have to go and live with Stephen, then."

"I don't know where you get it from."

"Well, perhaps we'll find out. Ha, ha!"

"Good lord, I didn't think of that."

They both laughed.

"Aren't you going to stay over?"

"No, I've got a ticket back to London. First class."

Jenna liked to go home, but she did not like to stay at home. Three or four hours were quite sufficient. Apart from Christmas, when she steeled herself for three days, a stay over was permissible only when strictly unavoidable. Staying at home any longer than that made her restless and depressed.

"You will ring me as soon as you get back, won't you?"

"Yes," said Jenna, acceding to the old ritual.

"Have you got food in, or shall I pack you something?"

"Mum!"

"Well, you need to look after yourself, darling. Now, a pot of tea before you go…"

Chapter 22

1628

The boy had absconded. It was not the first time that the Master of the College had alerted Sir Richard of the boy's wayward behaviour; he was excessively fond of the theatre and had taken to mixing with unsavoury elements from that milieu, spending his time in taverns, returning to college at all kinds of ungodly hours; but this was different: he had not been seen for a week. Even those of his fellows who, closest to him, normally helped him cover his tracks, admitted that, this time, he had confided in no-one.

"You'd better come with me, Thomas," said Sir Richard, preparing to go to London two weeks before his usual spring schedule.

Thomas caught Lady Anne's eye, her face a mask of anxiety. She nodded.

Four days later, they arrived in Marylebone, and the following morning Thomas Cheadle set out to question people in the places the boy was known to frequent. Generally, the people he spoke to were suspicious, uncooperative, satirical. In the yard of one tavern, he had to fend off a drunken bully who tried to manhandle him; in another, he judged it wise to leave hastily as he sensed the mood becoming aggressive. It was a tavern girl in Southwark, on the third day of his search, who at last gave him the clue he was looking for.

"He talked of going to Erith," she said. "There's a girl there, the daughter of a miller, with child by him."

The village of Erith, a small riverside port on the Kentish bank, was a two-hour journey, and Thomas Cheadle, accompanied by

Sir Richard, arrived there in the late forenoon. Once there, it was not difficult to find the boy's whereabouts.

"You fool!" said his father, confronting him. "Is this a fit place? Are these fit people for you to mix with? Do you intend to insult me, and bring shame to your family with this escapade?"

The boy withstood his father's assault with an open-faced manliness which Cheadle had not seen before, and which he secretly admired.

"She's with child," he said. "I'm the father."

"How can you be sure of that, you fool!"

The boy did not flinch.

"Besides, what of it? Take me to her father, I'll make a settlement. That's no doubt what they're in the game for."

"What do you have to say to me?" said the father, when he was brought in. He was a big man, with a spreading grey beard, wearing the leather apron of his trade. The daughter, who entered with him, was a comely girl, just showing with child. She went to stand by Richard, and he put his arm round her shoulder.

"You know who I am," said Sir Richard. "My son is of a considerable family, heir to a substantial estate, which he will forfeit if he persists in this nonsense. I'm prepared to make a generous settlement for the child's upbringing but there the connection must end, entirely, here and now, and my son will return with me."

"Well," said the miller, "you've spoken to a purpose and that must be considered, indeed. As for me, I care not for your estate or for your settlement, but if your son here, or my daughter here, is of a different mind, then let them speak, and I'll stand by what they say. But I think you'll find, sir, that your journey has been in vain."

"Well?" said Sir Richard, addressing the couple.

"We're already married, father. I must stay by my wife."

"You fool!" said Sir Richard, bitterly. "So be it. You know what to expect!" And with that he turned to go.

"Thomas," said the boy, touching his sleeve, "will you tell my mother that I am well, and that I intend to be happy. Tell her she isn't to worry."

Cheadle nodded and briefly squeezed the young man's hand.

"He will disinherit him," said Lady Anne.

"Yes," said Cheadle. "He instructed me to draw up papers to that effect."

"He offered to make a settlement, though?"

"Yes."

"And Richard refused."

"He did."

"Then I'm happy for him," she said.

It was the morning after Cheadle's return, alone, from London. The dawn was just beginning to form a liquid light at the window.

"He has bastards, you know," she continued. "Did you know that?" And then, after a moment, "I take it from your silence that you do."

She tipped his chin up to study his eyes for the truth.

"He makes provision for two children in London, one in Twickenham, one in Chertsey, both boys."

"So you see," she said, "does not his sin mitigate ours?"

"Do sins do cancel each other out?"

"I don't know. But if a man breaks his marriage vows, may not a woman?"

"Marriage vows are made not to a husband or a wife, but to God."

"And how if we marry, should he die before me? Will that atone for our sins?"

Thomas Cheadle smiled, "You must ask a scholar of divinity to tease that one out. For my own part, I care not so long as we may continue in them."

"Howsoever, let us make a vow now that we will marry if that day ever comes. Do you vow to me now, Thomas, before God, that you will take me as your wife, if ever you are able."

"Yes."

"And I make that vow to you."

"I should go," he said. "The house will be awake."

"Not yet," she murmured, softly, beguilingly, "not until you have given earnest of your vow."

Chapter 23

During her time at university, Jenna had not come out, but in the aftermath of her father's death, and recovering from a bout of clinical depression with a three month course of imipramine, she had felt a kind of reckless new energy for life and it had not been difficult to find girls to sleep with, though she pretended, as did they, that she was just high on life, doing it for kicks, for the hell of it, and as they said, girls together: the safest form of sex.

In the TV world, it was so common that you could come out without anyone batting an eyelid, but she had taken Gordon's advice and been discreet with the two or three girls she went out with during that time. Only Louisa, when they were splitting up, had threatened to 'out' Swatch to the tabloids, but then she had broken down in tears, begged for forgiveness, and promised to go off and take an overdose instead. Louisa was now a programme controller for Radio 2.

And then there was Eleanor. Eleanor was ten years older, and was a sculptor, and had a converted barn near Eynsford in Kent, where she had a studio, and a vegetable garden, and a herb garden, and two golden Labradors, and who made wonderful cakes and pastries. Eleanor, who was tall and graceful, and who was the gentlest and most passionate of lovers, and the most considerate of partners. They had lived together for three years and Eleanor had comforted her [when *Switch* finished and there was nothing else in the pipeline] and cosseted her and treated her at Harrods and Harvey Nichols [never settle for second best, darling!]. Eleanor was the person she had most loved, and who she still loved, but living with her had eventually driven her almost to the verge of insanity. They occasionally met for lunch in town, and Jenna had phoned her to tell her about *What's My Lineage*, though - and not without a sneaking feeling of guilt - she had omitted to tell her about Maisie.

It was a week after the trip to Reading that Maisie called. "Can you meet me up in town tomorrow? We can do lunch if you like."

Jenna felt a flaring of excitement, a distinct fluttering. "God, what am I like!" she said to herself. She went through her wardrobe to find an outfit: something seemingly natural, stunning, of course, but as if by chance.

They had lunch at Grants, a newly opened wine bar just off the Strand. Maisie was wearing a pale lemon cotton print summer frock, with delicious, almost eatable, red shoes.

They looked at the menu, decided on starters, side dish and salad, and ordered a bottle of Grenache Rose.

"Right," said Maisie. "Well, we haven't found any direct relations in Virginia, but our chap out there has been ferreting around, and he thinks he's found someone who knew your great grandfather at about the time America joined the first war."

"When was that? 1917?"

"Yes. Anyway, we think there may be a story there, because your great grandfather enlisted and went to France."

"Really!"

"So we think. So, what we're going to do is send you out there to meet the person who knew him. Meantime we'll track down his regiment and see where they went in France. If it's anywhere interesting, you know, that we can link him directly with, we'll then send you there and that will make a nice little story."

"A trip to France, too!"

"With any luck. So, we've set it up for America, on Tuesday, leaving the day after tomorrow. You can make that, can't you?"

"Yes."

The waiter came to take away the plates. They sipped the last glass of wine.

"Do you have to get back to work?" said Jenna.

"No, it's my afternoon off."

"Oh well, another glass of…"

"No, better not. I said I'd go over to see a friend in Kingston later. Better not get squiffy."

Don't be moody, Jenna said to herself, immediately, despite the disappointment, don't let it show. Thank God, I didn't ask her back, she reflected, which is what she would have done after another half glass of wine. Thank God she'd also resisted the immediate temptation of saying, *anyone special*?

"Coffee, then?"

"Ooh, yes please."

"Will I see you at the airport?"

"Oh I'm not going to the States," said Maisie. "I'd love to, but they've got too much on for me here."

"Oh," said Jenna, though the immediate pang was offset by Maisie putting her hand consolingly over hers. "Sorry!" she said. "You'll be all right, won't you?"

A little touch can do so much.

I forgive you, said Jenna to herself. I forgive you everything.

Chapter 24

London, October 1831

Of the two letters, posted by the two sisters, on the same day, from Beaumaris, only one, the letter Emily had sent to her guardian, Roger Harcourt, had reached its intended recipient.

The reason James Pennington had not received the letter penned by Harcourt's other ward, Isobel, and professing her undying attachment to him, was that it had been intercepted by, and was now in the possession of, Meg Liddle.

She had met the delivery boy quite by chance at the door of Pennington's lodgings, paid him the four pence required for the letter, and had then conveyed it to the close concealment of her bosom. A short time later, having climbed the five staircases to her attic room in Gooseberry Lane, she untied the ribbon and read it.

There was a very distant noise, as of a person turning around, uncomfortably, in the very confined space of an otherwise peaceful tomb. Meg heard it but chose to ignore it; she placed the letter at the bottom of her cabinet, and covered it with clothes.

"There," she said, "that'll do for you!"

Chapter 25

Jenna is travelling to Virginia, the voiceover will say when the programme is aired later in the year...

With her on the plane is John, a newly fledged assistant producer, who will also take some incidental camcorder footage during the journey. They will be met, in Richmond, by Sam Grimes, a producer from a newly formed American production company who are dealing with the US side of the project to comply with regulations, who is in charge of the itinerary over there.

The usual trial of the airport is compounded by an air controllers' work to rule in France which has had knock-on effects across the globe, it seems. The food outlets and bistros are packed; people stand patiently watching the departures and arrivals screens as if their individual attentiveness will have some effect in unlocking the intricate scramble. Jenna buys a thick novel in W.H. Smith, one of those modern romances spawned by the Grail legend, is nodded to and stared after by a young man outside Dixons, obviously, she surmises, a *Switch* watcher in days of yore, and finally settles, for what turns out to be a two-hour delay, on the corner of a bench.

Any excitement she might have felt in days gone by regarding air travel is now long gone.

The whole airport, it seems, has become a walk-through store, a bemusing through-the-looking-glass world: the different franchises, booze, perfumes, i-phones, digital cameras other luxury goods, seen through a prismatic wilderness.

At last the flight is called, and Jenna sits with the usual tension, the usual irrational fear that focuses on the moment of take-off, and then intensifies for ninety seconds, with the dragging up of the undercarriage and through the process of banking and levelling, and then magically disappears as the steady drone of safe peaceful aeroplane flight prevails.

For a moment, the lights of London flicker below, seen at an odd angle over the wing as the plane banks again, and she thinks of Maisie, somewhere down there, and feels ineffably sad. Maisie, seeing her friend in Kingston, perhaps. A pang of jealousy flickers.

Gloomy, gloomy, gloomy
Don't want to be here. Don't want to be here.
Moody moody moody.

"Would you like a drink this evening, madam?"

"Gin and tonic, please."

"Gin and tonic? Lovely. Ice?"

"Thanks."

"So, Jenna," says John, sitting beside her, "can we just run by the schedule?"

She sighs inwardly. Typical of the young producer, brisk, keen, efficient, desperate to get everything right. Terribly tedious.

He consults his clip board.

"Land in JFK 0500 hours, time for a snack, flight to Richmond at 8am, hotel in Maybridge. Start work the following morning. A bit of time to relax," he concludes with a laugh.

Good. She takes a sip and hopes he will now find something else with which to preoccupy himself for the rest of the flight.

"Look," he said, putting the clipboard aside, "I suppose we're going to be pretty much, you know, together over the next few days, and I know what it's like sometimes, so, cards on the table, I'd just like to absolutely reassure you that you don't have to worry about anything with me."

"Worry?"

"Yes, you know, I expect you find men coming on to you, you know, all the time, but with me, well…" He held his hands up, letting that finish the sentence.

"I'm very glad to hear it."

"No. Well, as a matter of fact, I've just got engaged."

"Congratulations."

"Thank you. Yes. She's called Michelle actually. Well, we've been living together for, oh, you know, about eighteen months, then decided to take the big step."

"How exciting."

He went on, seeming not to have picked up on her irony. "Well, it'll probably be a while yet before we, you know... but it's the commitment, isn't it?" Here he produced his wallet and slipped out a photograph. "That's her in Xante last summer?"

"She's very pretty."

"Have you ever been there? Xante, I mean."

"No, no I haven't."

"Pity. Very beautiful. We'll definitely go back there. Anyway, yes, we've got a flat in Islington, tiny. We'd like to move out, you know where there's a bit more space and a few fields, somewhere Michelle can keep a couple of ponies, sort of thing, you know, but, you know, it'll probably be a couple of years. Actually, her parents offered to put us up, they've got a four-bedroom detached in Ilford. Might make it easier to save money that way, but you know, in-laws and so on. You can't imagine being relaxed, in bed sort of thing, can you?"

"No. Is she particularly noisy?"

John laughed with pleased embarrassment.

"You should have seen her reaction when I told her I was coming out on this trip with you."

"Oh yes?"

"Well, you know, just a teensy-weensy bit of jealousy I did detect."

"Well I expect you reassured her just as you've reassured me."

"Tried to Jenna, tried to. Not always the easiest of things! She's a bit in awe of you, I think, you know, *Country Retreats* and that. She's an avid watcher."

"She didn't used to watch Swivel and Swatch, did she?"

"What's that?"

"Never mind. You should have just told her I was gay."

"Oh, I wouldn't..."
It was a moment before he saw that it was not a joke.
"You're...?"
"Gay, yes. I thought it was common knowledge."
"Oh."

One of the unlooked-for advantages of being gay, it sometimes struck Jenna, was that it could provide a very effective conversation stopper.

The momentary awkwardness was interrupted by the arrival of a trolley, offering the first of their in-flight meals. She declined, John accepted, opening each pre-sealed packet carefully, and then tucking in like one enjoying a special treat. When the empty cartons had been removed, and tea and coffee and further drinks served, John put on his headphones and tuned into the in-flight movie, and despite his habit of laughing aloud without realising how absurd and irritating this was to those sitting around him, she was able to feel a certain degree of seclusion.

She decided against the novel, whose prose, to judge from the first chapter which she had read in the airport, was exceedingly turgid, and instead, took her i-pod from her bag and listened, first of all, to the prelude of *Traviata*, which she had uploaded the previous evening. The plangent strings, dreamy and wistful, led, via a descending scale into the oom-pa-pa-pa background and then the simple almost child-like tune followed its progress to a warbling pirouette of an end-phrase, and then repeated, this time with delightful tripping, dancing elaborations behind the melody, and then to the coda, and then over. She played it again, thinking of Maisie, and marvelled at how quickly a line of music can become imbued with the sense of a person, a nostalgia for the face and the hair and the scent, a rich infatuation.

She selected next the Adagio from Mahler's fifth, the most sublime piece of music ever written, she sometimes said, not as an informed judgement, but in keeping with the sublime feelings she experienced listening to it, and again she thought of Maisie. How beautiful it would be to be sharing this music with her, to be immersed together in such a bath of feeling. She pictured a large soft bed, herself and Maisie holding each other; it was a fantasy of luxurious self-indulgence to compare with the dry air and the steady dim light of the aeroplane.

Beside her, John was now asleep, still with his earphones on, but with his head lolling to one side, thankfully not towards her. She pressed the *attention* button and called for another gin and tonic, and tried to remember why it was she was here. Someone in America who could throw some light on someone who died ninety years ago. All this time and effort and expense to get something that would produce probably less than a minute of airtime. Was it worth it? At this moment in time, stuck in a droning air-conditioned cigar tube over the Atlantic, all considerations of career and publicity, all the things Bex, her agent, was so keen to promote, seemed absurd.

At some point, she must have drifted off; she woke at ten past two, still with half a glass of gin and tonic in her hand. John's earpiece had come adrift and a thin tinny music was coming from it. She reached forward and turned off his i-pod, and then, for want of anything else to do with it, she swigged off the rest of the gin and tonic.

The rest of the night was filled with thin sleep, shallow incoherent shreds of dream, dislocated thoughts, and increasingly unreal fantasies about Maisie, until at last, at about four, she woke up again. Someone, two or three aisles behind, was snoring, not loudly, just enough to be maddening; her mouth was dry, her head light, the taste of gin still acrid in her throat.

Time has stood still, she said to herself. This plane is hanging over the clouds, going nowhere. I'm stuck forever in a void. Nothing will ever be real again.

When they brought round the breakfast, she fell into the trap, with John alongside her, each of them peeling open their cartons, simultaneously. A small piece of bacon, a mini-sausage, a spoonful of scrambled egg – it tasted delicious. A spongy bun with butter and marmalade. Coffee, and then more coffee.

In Richmond, she found herself in the hotel room with a view down over windy streets, and traffic. There were some diners, some bars, a liquor store, but no shops to speak of, just a mall two miles out of town. She slept for three hours, watched some television, then telephoned her mother and told her everything was fine. She wondered about calling Maisie but decided against it. At six, John knocked on the door and asked her if she wanted to go out for something to eat. It was clear that he, too, was feeling out of sorts, jet-lagged, bored and homesick. They walked two blocks, had a pizza and a couple of beers, and talked – a confederacy of the dejected.

"I phoned her up but there was no reply," he said. "Makes you worry, doesn't it, you know, when you're so far away. You think anything could have happened. Though sometimes, she does it to punish me," he added, with a forlorn smile, "you know, not picking up."

"Treats you mean to keep you keen," she replied, reflecting on the sad complications of living-together relationships, but at the same time thinking of Maisie and her mysterious friend in Kingston.

Chapter 26

London, October 1831

"This is a filthy world," said Pennington, to his friend, Kit, in Cutler's tavern. "A filthy abomination of a dog world. Worse than that. A world not fit for dogs. A rat-infested sewer of a world. A vile running sore, pox-ridden, shit-besmirched, pus-dribbling, putrefying dog world."

"You've had dog world once," said Kit, who did not like to interrupt his own enjoyment of Pennington's railing except for such technical corrections as this.

It was seven o'clock in the evening, and the nine hours which had lapsed since he had parted from Roger Harcourt, had not assuaged his bitterness.

"If I had my way," Pennington continued, now on a new tack, "I'd pack the whole excremental tribe of them into a dung cart and tip them into the stews, and drown them in horse piss; I'd make them drink their own effluent, and set hungry rats loose in their beds while they're beasting it with their foul caterwauling, powder cheeked, maggot-riddled whores…"

"Have a drink," said Kit, in this momentary hiatus, "Cool your chaps, dampen down the smoke."

"Damn them all," said Pennington, before at last taking Kit's advice.

There followed a period of profound melancholy introspection which lasted for some five minutes, the time it took to drain down, in slow considered mouthfuls, the contents of a pewter tankard.

"So," said Kit, after calling over the tavern wench for replenishment, "to what tiny ripple of disturbance to the otherwise smooth and silvery current of your existence do we owe this, your most recent tirade against mankind?"

Still silence from Pennington.

"Or is it some more particular adversary who has offended the delicacy of your sensibility?"

"Today," announced Pennington, now leaning over the table, and clenching a fist which he held ready to bring down on its surface, "Today, that vicious enemy of all that is decent, Roger Harcourt came to see me."

"Say no more!" said Kit with heavy irony. "Let all such unwelcome social visits be punishable by death."

"He came to bribe me. To corrupt me. To make me eat the rat poison of betrayal."

"Forgive me if this is an utterly irrelevant and wayward supposition, but was the subject this impossible attempt to puncture your unassailable integrity, by any chance his niece?"

"His ward, not his niece."

"His ward, then."

"He wants me to hand her letters over to him. He offered me five guineas."

"Ask ten."

"I did."

"You villain."

"Only to provoke him. Besides, I haven't had any letters."

"Get Meg to counterfeit one. Can she write?"

"I doubt it."

"Write it yourself."

"Don't trifle with me, you ignorant donkey! Can't you see what a disgusting cesspit this has thrown me into?"

"So what are you going to do?"

"You know he never paid me for her portrait."

"Well, in the circumstances..."

"Today he said he'd pay me forty guineas for it."

"Very fair, I would have thought. Has he had it?"

"No."

"Well, send it to him."

"That's your advice is it?"

"Not only is it my advice, it's a condition of our continuing friendship, if you set any value on it."

"I don't."

"Very well then, do as you like. Die in poverty, die hungry, die any death you please, but never ask for my advice again."

"He wants to buy it so that he can destroy it."

"Oh, I see."

"The venomous parasite, that he is, the contagious dropsical…"

"Don't start that again, old chap, haven't got all night. we need to think about this."

"What is there to think about?"

"Well, as you yourself once said, an artist should not have a sentimental attachment to his own work."

"Did I say that?"

"Yes."

"Well, it's true. Great art assumes a life of its own, quite independent of its maker or its subject."

"Quite so, I agree with you entirely. But leaving such loftiness of thought aside, if you have no sentimental attachment to the portrait of Isobel Harcourt, why should you not accept forty guineas for it, and bid it farewell."

"I could do with the money," said Harcourt glumly.

"Of course you could. You have to live. If forty guineas was the price you agreed, conclude the bargain and be done with it."

"Damn it all, let's have another drink," said Pennington, now seeming to throw off the shackles of his melancholy. "Let's drink to friendship, Kit, for when all's said and done, what better thing can a man aspire to than to comradeship?"

"Comradeship!" said Kit, chiming in with the toast.

"The man who is my friend is my brother," said Pennington.

"Buy me a small one," said Meg Liddle, who had just joined the company.

"Listen to this, Meg," said Kit. "A man is offered ten guineas to hand over a letter, what does he do?"

"That depends on who the letter is from."

"This is ten guineas, Meg. And what's a letter but a piece of paper with ink marks on it?"

"I'm sure I don't know."

"Leave her out of it, Kit. That pretty head, whatever it was made for, and I don't pretend to know, was not made for moral dilemmas."

"Leave off," said Meg.

As the evening drew on and the company became merry, Pennington allowed himself to be distracted from his dark preoccupation with Roger Harcourt. Kit, who had a bookshop in Fennery Lane, and numbered among his clients several down-at-heels poets who lodged in the neighbourhood, was usually furnished, from his day's business. with an amusing tale or two, and he was a fine mimic.

"What do you mean, you don't have a copy of my book!" He was imitating the poet George Bancroft, who had a high reedy voice, and a very inflated opinion of his own standing in the world of letters. *"You don't keep my book! What sort of bookshop do you call yourself!"*

Pennington laughed and felt himself completely at one with the company. There were certain states of inebriation in which the world seemed to become a completely harmonious place, brightly lit and full of heart-warming mirth.

"So," said Kit, at last, "has the melancholy fit run its course?"

"Absolutely," said Pennington, with a slight but noticeable slurring of his words.

"Better get you home," said Kit.

"No, listen. Listen! I'll none of it. Here is his card. I rip it once. I rip it twice. And let that be an end of it. I'll none of his filthy money."

"Are you going back with him?" he asked Meg.

"Not me. He sometimes turns nasty when he's like this."

"Right. Here we go then. Come on, old chap. Put your arm over my shoulder, that's it, and I'll walk you home like a lover and his lass!"

Chapter 27

James Pennington awoke in his armchair at an hour which, having taken stock of the surrounding circumstances, the amount of noise from the street, or lack of it, the light at the window, or lack of it, he guessed to be somewhere in the region of two o'clock in the morning. Acknowledging the main cause of his untimely wakefulness to be directly linked to the amount of liquor he had consumed the previous evening, he dragged himself up and sought the means of relieving his bladder.

This accomplished, he picked his way through the darkness of the room to his bed, determined to lose himself in oblivion once more until the cheering images of the morning brought him back to the world of the living.

Further sleep, however, was tantalisingly elusive, and amidst such insistent thoughts as coursed maddeningly through the circle of his brain, the most maddeningly insistent was the one which put forward the simple proposition that forty guineas was a lot of money.

Besides the settling of petty debts, forty guineas would go a long way to paying for a trip to Paris, or to the country, or the mountains and lakes of Cumbria, anywhere to get himself away from London, away from the hole he seemed to have got himself stuck in ever since that ill-fated venture which had ended at the King's Head in Dartford.

Kicking aside the blanket at last, he fumbled about, amongst his brushes and knives and paints, for a tinder, and lit two candles and a lamp. Then, he pulled out, from behind the dozen other framed canvasses where he had put it away, the portrait of Isobel Harcourt, set it on an easel in the middle of the room, and drew up his armchair to look at it.

It was his intention to look at it, much in the way Kit had suggested, as a business proposition. To test his own ruthlessness. To exorcise any attachment that might still linger. To exculpate himself. To prepare a clear route by which the forty guineas which Roger Harcourt could well afford would find its way into his pocket.

The effect, however, was quite the opposite. It was not just a painting of a woman; it was thousands of brush strokes, each one deftly applied, a composition of light and shade, each tone and colour lovingly blended. It was Isobel Harcourt, and the eyes which looked out at him, astonishingly bright and with their own soft yearning were the eyes of a woman he had loved and who had loved him.

A host of half remembered conversations whispered in his ears; moments of tenderness and trust, moments of gentleness and revelation plucked at his heart like the strings of a Spanish guitar. The green gown, the black chapeau with the feather, the gloves.

On the day of their proposed elopement, she had arrived, as if for a sitting, wearing the outfit. Then she had changed into her travelling clothes, and later, when he returned from Dartford alone, the outfit had been put hastily away in a trunk just as her portrait had been hidden away behind the others. Things he did not want to be reminded of.

In an ideal world, James Pennington would love Isobel Harcourt every bit as much as he had several times, and with genuine passion, told her he did. What that ideal world might be like, he had no true idea, but he knew it was not the world he lived in. In the spell of the moment, in the influence of the charm, in the magical aura she was everything to him that a woman possibly could be, but the magic ended, the moment passed, the spell dissolved...!

Crossing the river at Westminster was a delirious moment of escape; from Southwell to Deptford, a throng of intoxicating thoughts danced attendance on them; from Deptford to

Shooters Hill, in calmer mood, they admired the open perspective of Blackheath, and then the villages of Kent, all laid before them as in the landscape of a dream: Kidbrooke, Falconwood, Welling, Bexley, Crayford, Dartford.

At Dartford, with the onset of dusk, the darkest cloud of apprehension came over him. What on earth was he doing! What possible life together could the future hold? After a few months of roaming in France, what manner of living could he offer her that would not become, as much for her as for him, grotesque?

In the morning, he made an excuse for delay, some business he had to deal with at the post before leaving England. It was a moment of elemental cowardice, of fear even greater than any rational objection, of moral paralysis.

The next Dover coach was a six hour wait. Before that time was up, Harcourt had arrived, with two strong arms in his company. He made a show of pushing them aside; they pinioned him, until the girl was safely stowed in her guardian's coach.

And to his shame, he felt an immense relief.

Her portrait now, even as the first glimmer of light seeped through the shutters, revived all those headlong feelings as if she were standing in the room before him.

He could not part with it.

Not for forty guineas. Not for a hundred. It was his work, and his soul was in his work – he could not pass it on simply to be destroyed. Not for any price.

But there was something he could do. It suddenly struck him with all the simplicity that great ideas have. There was an absolutely straightforward way he could keep the portrait and have the forty guineas which Harcourt had put on offer. He quickly put the portrait back in its place behind the other frames, then donned his cloak and hat, and set out in the first cold light of dawn in the direction of Gooseberry Lane.

Chapter 28

"So, Jenna," said the large man, with overbearing familiarity, "this is what we have lined up for you."

He thinks he's a big shot, thought Jenna.

He was thirty-five. Wearing a cream suit, big watch, big rings, a tortoise shell tie-pin and matching cufflinks. Lapel badge which said: Clinton Salmon, Mayridge Media Corp., Senior Production Consultant. Big shot, everything about him said. Catching a glimpse of John, whom Salmon had so far ignored, she could tell that he had formed the same impression.

The idea is we drive up to Mayville, see what we can put together. The guy in question would be your great grandfather, right? So, we're tracking him down through army records, follow up with the war-graves commission, then your people in London will fly you out there, see where he's buried, where he died etc.

"Sounds like a plan."

"Surprised they haven't done all that before now," said John, in the back seat of the car, as Salmon took a call on his mobile.

"Just go with the flow," said Jenna.

It was a two-hour drive, into the foothills of the Allegheny Mountains. From the driving seat, Salmon threw back knowledgeable comments about the terrain, Peters Mountain, the old plantations, the Mason-Dixon Line and other historical titbits to impress tourists.

The town was spread over the slope of a hillside with tree-lined avenues and single storey wood-built houses. They parked the car, and John, with Ray, Clinton Salmon's technical man, began to unpack the equipment, whilst Salmon approached the house and knocked on the door. An elderly woman came into the porch and peered uneasily towards the camera which the boys were setting up, as Salmon talked to her.

It soon became evident that it was not going to plan; the woman was suspicious of the camera and became defensive. Salmon insisted that they'd spoken to her before, but she seemed to think now that they were from the tax department or some other government agency.

"Why you asking all these questions?" she said.

She softened when Jenna began to speak to her but the woman didn't understand the programme. How did one explain the current English fascination with family trees, lineage and ancestry which went with the plethora of websites set up to make such information available.

At last, however, she began to tell the story that Salmon insisted he had got from her before.

"Three of them went that I remember, Jem Jeffers, Bill Tooms – he was my daddy – and Lawson Shaw. Only two of them came back, that was my daddy and Jem Jeffers."

"So, Lawson Shaw was lost in action?"

"No ma'am."

"No?"

The old woman shook her head slowly.

"But you said he never came back," interjected Salmon.

"I said he never came back. I mean he never came back here. Went out to California, his wife and his boy followed a couple of years later."

Salmon cussed and turned away to walk to the car.

Keep smiling, said Jenna to herself. "So, you would have remembered Sam, then?" she asked.

"Oh sure."

"Sam would have been my grandfather."

"That so?"

"Yes. What was he like? Do you remember?"

"Well, he was kinda small. But then he was only a kid you know, say, four years old when I was eight or nine. There was a lot of kids about at that time, I just remember Lawson Shaw's boy as one of them, you know."

"Thank you," said Jenna.

She turned to Salmon and shrugged her shoulders.

"OK," said Salmon. "OK, we've got enough here, now."

"Thank you again," said Jenna to the old woman.

"Well, ma'am, I hope you find him. Be around ninety years old, by now, just a little less than me."

That was a disaster," said Jenna, in the car.

"Sloppy research," said John, like an old pro.

Salmon, however, shrugged it off. "It's as I said. He went to France. There's still a story there. We'll find out from military records where he served. I'll get the boys on it soon as I'm back in the office."

They arrived back outside the hotel.

"Hey guys, pick you up about seven, take you out to eat? Don't object, all on expenses."

"I don't think that was a question," said Jenna as they went through the lobby.

"Well, safety in numbers."

They ate in a small Chinese diner two blocks away from the hotel. Salmon, who had now expunged all trace of the day's farce from his memory, was in good form, loud and hearty. Later, he insisted they have a night-cap in the hotel bar, and began a series of stories which required, in the telling, frequently reaching over to touch Jenna's wrist with his fingertip.

"Will you excuse me?" she said, opting for the respite of a visit to the washroom.

When she returned, Salmon was standing. "Hey, look hey, I'm sorry, I gotta go, see you in the morning, guys."

He left brusquely.

"What happened?"

"Well, he was coming on a bit strong, wasn't he?"

"I can look after myself, John!"

"Yes, I know."

"So, what happened?"

"He asked me if I hadn't got something else to do."
"And...?"
"Well..."
"Did you tell him I was gay?"
"Yes...I thought..."
"John!"
"Are you annoyed with me?"
"Yes."
"But why?"
"Because I can look after myself thank you very much!"
John sat back, looking crumpled, down in the mouth.
"I'll forgive you, but only on one condition."
"What's that?" said John, warily.
"That you buy me another drink."
"What, at these prices?"
"Yes, at these prices."
"All right, then it's a deal!"

The following morning there was a phone call from Salmon's P.A. Military records, she told them, showed that Lawson Shaw's regiment didn't see action in the war. They were held in reserve in a training camp in Belgium, then Armistice was declared. That sort of thing happened apparently.

"So, no story at all."
"No story."
"This gets better and better."
She phoned Simon.
"Never mind. A cul-de-sac can usually be turned into something interesting. Even if we get a couple of minutes."
"Expensive couple of minutes."
"Well, that's the way it is sometimes. We'll see what you've got and get the writers to do you some script. We can film that back here."
"Right, we come back then?"
She saw John awaiting the response eagerly.
"Yes, I guess so."
"OK, then, see you in a couple of days."

She looked at John. He was already on his mobile to Michelle.

Jenna decided to give way to the temptation of sending a quick text message to Maisie. *Back tomorrow or Wednesday. Do you fancy lunch later in the week? J.*

She pressed the send button before wisdom got the better of her.

Chapter 29

London, October 1831

It was not uncommon for there to be noise during the night in the lodging house where Meg Liddle had her small attic room. Sometimes a brawl on the street outside, or a drunken row disturbed the rest of those inmates who had managed to find some respite from the world in sleep. Sometimes the angry shriek of a woman's voice and the growl of a man's denoted some disagreement over a transaction that had taken place between them; sometimes the insistent clacking of a rickety bedstead denoted the nature of such a transaction in its progress. The coming and going of people seemed to know no distinction of night or day, and Meg Liddle, lying on her bolster, with the thin woollen cover pulled up to her chin and her ears, seldom slept deeply enough to be unaware of the padding of feet up the bare wooden stairs and the padding of feet down the bare wooden stairs: visitor to Jenny on the second floor; same visitor departing half an hour later: old Stritch on the third floor going out to find liquor; old Stritch returning, sometimes with a companion to share his bottle. Without counting, she knew the number of foot-treads that led to each floor, and if any strayed further, even by a single step, than the final landing, she was out of bed and ready with a cudgel at an arm's length from the door before those footsteps had progressed to the half-way point of the staircase.

The swiftness of the footsteps which began their ascent of the first flight at five o'clock in the morning, light as it was, was sufficient to cause Meg to open her eyes; by the time those same steps had reached the third landing, she was alert in every fibre of her body, and by the time she heard them begin the final flight, her nerves thrilled with sudden alarm. By the time her door burst open, she was ready with her cudgel and that same cudgel had just begun its downward trajectory with as much force as her slight frame could make, when she recognised the face of her intruder.

"For heaven's sake, Meg," said James Pennington, shielding his face with his arm, as the blow, somewhat abated, struck his shoulder.

The little gasp of shock and regret, blended in a choked scream, which emitted from her throat might well have been taken, by the residents of that house, as that of another sound with which they were well familiar, but if any prurient ears were listening, any repetition they might be expecting did not come, only the sound of muffled voices.

"What are you doing here at this…"

"Ssh, Meg. Quick get your clothes on and come with me."

"What's going on?"

"Never mind. Get your clothes on. Here I'll help you. Does this go over your head?"

"Leave me be. It's all right. I can dress myself. What's all the flaming hurry!"

A moment later she was being led, by the hand, and at a pace much greater than that which her own legs were made for, down the stairs and out onto the street. In ten minutes, and without the pace having slackened a jot, she was being led, almost dragged, up the stairs to Pennington's studio.

"Right, Meg, get your clothes off," said Pennington.

"Blimey," said Meg, "you're keen, aren't you!"

"No, not that!"

"Put your clothes on, take your clothes off, I wish you'd make your mind up."

"Put this on, Meg," he said, handing her the bodice and skirt of a green riding habit. "I want to paint you."

"Give me a bit of privacy, then."

"Privacy, what do you want privacy for?"

"Well, just give me some room, then."

Chapter 30

"Stay still."

"I'm trying to stay still."

"Try harder."

"I've been still for four hours. It's more than's humanly possible."

"Stop squeaking. If you move now you'll ruin the whole thing."

Meg strained every fibre of her being to remain still.

"All right," said Pennington, at last. "We'll have a break. Get your proper clothes on and go down to the coffee shop and see what they've got. Some pastries or something, and a flagon of coffee. Here's a shilling."

"Can't I go in these clothes," she said, "like a proper fine lady?"

He stood at the window and watched her cross the road. It could be her, he said to himself, with a curious flicker of pleasure. It could be her.

"Right," said Pennington, later, "that's it. I've done enough for today. No more. I'll finish it off tomorrow."

The main part of the portrait was complete. The dress, with all its folds and shadows, the chapeau with its feathers, the hair arranged beneath. Only the face remained, and that, of course, was going to be Isobel's face, not Meg's. He had needed a model for the figure and the posture, it would not have done simply to copy the original, but the face would have to be done from memory, and that promised its own bitter-sweet pleasure.

"Have I been a good girl today?"

Recognising the would-be seductiveness of the cadence, Pennington turned to see Meg in her dishabille, the smock, arranged with studied negligence, to offer glimpses within.

In spite of himself, Pennington's blood stirred.

"There," she said, a little later, "Did she ever please you as I do?"

"No," Pennington acquiesced.

No, it was true. Whatever Harcourt might have surmised he had not debauched his niece.

At Dartford, though they had shared a room they had not shared a bed. *I am perfectly ready,* Isobel said, *and as soon as we reach France I shall become your wife.* What miserable scruple had he invented to delay that consummation? He shuddered to think what mockery he would have suffered at the hands of Kit if he had admitted it, but he could no more have made love to Isobel Harcourt that night than he could have to a marble statue.

Meg was a willing and uncomplicated lover. Her vanity was easily satisfied; she did not ask for a great deal in return other than to be wanted a little bit, and to be kept warm.

Sometimes the familiar wantonness was welcome and he could lose himself briefly in the simple pleasure of flesh; sometimes it palled. And he suspected that, at the least provocation or absence, she would quickly find her way into another man's bed.

He got up from the bed, and lighting a candle, took out the original portrait of Isobel Harcourt, then sat to look at it.

"The most desirable woman", Kit had once said, during a session at Cutler's, "is always the one you cannot have."

The fascination of Isobel Harcourt had been, at first, just that; in the setting of Evesham Place, she was not just a beautiful girl but a daughter of wealth and privilege, utterly unattainable yet tantalisingly near; later, when she had come unchaperoned to his studio, that had been replaced, or perhaps just conjoined, by the sense of danger, playing with fire.

The painting embodied some idyll of patrician refinement, a sense of the power of wealth to be comfortable and beautiful and self-pleasing. How will anyone see this painting in the future, he wondered. How would they see him, if at all? A man who had prostituted his talent to glorify wealth, rank, inherited privilege?

He remembered that his father had once railed, like him, against injustice and inequality, against a world that crushed the aspirations of the free man unless he had the backing of money, and yet was it not the truth that he was simply and fatefully attracted to that which he despised?

"Why is it always her?" The voice was Meg's but it could have been the thought in his own head. "What about me?"

He turned to look at her, surprised by the animation in her voice.

"You make me wear her clothes. You paint me as if I'm her. You take me into your bed and let me do things that would make my grandmother turn over in her grave yet here you sit, in the middle of the night, gazing at her."

"It's not what you think," said Pennington, wearily.

"And how do you know what I think, when you never bother to listen, and never even bother to notice I exist."

"Meg!" Said Pennington, "My pretty fool! What's brought all this on?"

"Never mind what's brought this on when you never bother to notice what brings anything on!"

"I don't know what you're talking about."

"How should you know what I'm talking about when you never bother to know anything I'm talking about."

Pennington acknowledged that Meg had found an irrefutable rhetoric for counteracting any argument. He also acknowledged that she had worked herself up into a fine lather of a temper.

"Look," he said at last, "we can't go on like this all night, maybe it would be better if you just went home."

"Oh, I'll go home all right," she said, pulling on her skirt and shoes, "and don't think it's my fault if I never sit still for you again!"

"I'll walk half way with you, shall I?"

"You'll not walk half way with me, not if I've anything to do with it, you'll not walk half way, nor quarter of the way, nor any part of the way, or it'll be the last time you do."

By now she was fully dressed and was reaching for her cloak and bonnet.

Pennington judged that it was best to sit out the rest of the storm in silence, and a short time later, with the slam of the inner door still ringing in his ears and the slam of the outer door echoing distantly, he was left alone.

Meg made her way down Jennyfield Lane, then turned into Vinegar Gardens and began to pick her way through the maze of tiny streets which led to Gooseberry Lane.

"Are you looking for business?" asked a man stepping out of the shadows on the corner of Flinders Square.

"After business, sweetheart?" asked another, just by the lodging house in Gooseberry Lane.

She swept by them both and made her way up the five flights of stairs to her room. There she drew her box from under the bed and cast all the contents aside until she held in her hand the letter which she had intercepted two days before.

"This is your fault," she said, speaking to the letter quite as venomously as she had spoken to James Pennington half an hour earlier. "This is all your fault!"

Chapter 31

The following morning, Meg Liddle slipped out of the doorway of her lodging house in Gooseberry Lane, wrapped her cloak tightly about her, and set out in the direction of Sparrowhill. It was eight o'clock, and a damp September morning, with an evil smelling mist over the Ludwell ditch sending cold fingers to linger in the air along all the adjacent streets. Avoiding Jennyfield Lane, for her present errand was such that she had no wish to bump into James Pennington, she crossed Tannery Square, then doubled back along Flinders Alley until she reached Bishopsfield Corner. From here, looking back towards the river, the dome of St Pauls was visible, with other spires of the city and chimneys and mill stacks pumping brown smoke into an already dirty sky.

Evesham Place was just a short distance from the park gates on Sparrowhill. It was a quiet square, with a central garden surrounded by wrought-iron railings and crossed by paths, with elegant town houses facing it on each side. In one corner of the lawn, a nurse sat with a perambulator under the shelter of a group of small trees but otherwise the square was empty.

It was not the first time she had stood on this spot.

On the other occasion, several months earlier, she had latched onto a young lad of eight or nine who was passing by. "What's your name, snapper?"

"Tommy, miss," replied the boy, who had learned in his short life that it was probably best to assume that all people had authority over him.

"Tommy what?"

"Tommy Slight."

"Well, Tommy Slight, how would you like to earn tuppence?"

Tommy simply nodded, the degree or manner of how he would like such a thing being quite indefinable.

"Go over to number seven, where Mr Harcourt lives, and deliver this note," she said, placing a folded piece of paper in his hands, "Go on, be sharp, and don't try to read it."

The latter admonition was in no danger of being ignored, for besides his natural inclination towards obedience, Tommy Slight could not read. Had he been tempted to unfold the note, however, and had he suddenly been blessed with the gift of letters, the meaningless hieroglyphs would have translated themselves into this brief message: *mind out for your niece she has run off with mr pennington on the post coach to dartford then dover from a wellwisher.*

On the present occasion, rather more than tuppence being in question, she went directly to the side entrance of number seven herself and pulled the cord. A bell sounded deep within and after half a minute a maid came to the door, opened it and looked her up and down.

"I've brought a message for Mr Harcourt," she said.

The maid looked her up and down again, and for a moment Meg was tempted to enquire as to whether the maid thought herself in any way superior, and if so on what grounds, but she resisted.

"It's something Mr Harcourt will be very curious about," she said instead.

A look passed across the maid's face as if to question her presumption of knowledge about her master, but she stepped back and let Meg pass by. "You'd better come in," she said, taking her to a small scullery near the main kitchen. "I'll call Mr Mobbes. He usually deals with such things. Who shall I say…"

"Miss Liddle."

"And the business…?"

"Just tell him it's to do with a letter. He'll know what it's about."

Chapter 32

"I would like you to examine the contents of this letter," said Roger Harcourt to Septimus Fairhurst, physician and Magistrate, the doctor who had attended his ward, Isobel, during her illness in the spring.

The doctor put on his spectacles, sat at his desk, and began to read the first of the three handwritten sheets which Harcourt had handed to him. As he read, he nodded considerately, grunting and making a series of gravelly noises in his throat.

"The infatuation is no less," he commented.

"Sadly not."

"Increased, if anything. It seems that absence has only served to intensify the confusion of feelings it was intended to remove."

"According to her sister, she continues to give cause for concern."

"Indeed."

"My fear is that her prolonged stay in Anglesey will only serve to worsen her condition."

"Then you intend to bring her home?"

"That is part of my intention."

"Indeed. And how may I be of assistance?"

"It is my opinion that her interests might best be served by a period of confinement where she may be properly cared for. And that, of course, is where your assistance is required. The matter is somewhat delicate. Isobel is nineteen, nearly twenty. At the age of twenty-one she will inherit a share of her father's estate. This, of course, is partly why it was so important to protect her from the predatory attentions of a man such as James

Pennington. If by reasons of incapacity she is unable to manage her affairs, it will fall to me as her guardian to manage them for her. It must be absolutely clear that I am acting in her best interests, and not from any selfish motive."

The doctor nodded and allowed himself a moment for thought. "It must be established," he said, at last, "that the young woman is a danger to herself or poses a danger to others."

Harcourt nodded towards the letter which Septimus still held in his hand. "Is further proof needed?"

The doctor skimmed over the letter again. *Worth more to me than life itself... gladly sacrifice all that I hold most dear...give myself to you body and soul...*

"The language is extreme in places," said the doctor.

"I should like you to write a letter of recommendation."

"But without seeing her, without examining her?"

"Would you expect to find anything that is not implicit in that letter?"

"Is there any evidence that she harms herself or abuses herself in any way?"

'Abuses herself?'

'Yes,' said the doctor. He looked up towards Harwood for a response, but could not sustain his look.

"What sort of evidence?"

The doctor shuffled uncomfortably. "Perhaps her sister might have observed or suspected..."

"God knows. Probably. How am I to know such things?"

"It is important to have some definite er..."

"Say yes then."

"But..."

"Say yes. Now I think of it, her sister has mentioned... well, for God sake, one tries to keep these things private out of a sense of shame on her behalf, but yes, though I shudder to admit it, yes. There, now you have it from me, and I hope you're satisfied.

"My dear Harcourt, it's not a question of my satisfaction."

"I'm relying on you, If anything should happen to her, I would hold you personally responsible. I'll expect to hear from you by, shall we say tomorrow morning?"

Dr Fairhurst returned to his chambers in Grantham Row, arriving just as a gloomy twilight was settling about the house. His housekeeper, Mrs Bryant, brought him a light supper of mutton and boiled potatoes, and then retired, leaving him to his own company and the silence of the house. The rooms were modestly, even sparsely furnished, and in fact, apart from the study, the small dining room and his own bedchamber, the main rooms in the house were scarcely used from one month to the next. He had a niece in Lowestoft – the daughter of a sister dead now more than fifteen years – but no other family, and he had always been a man of acquaintances rather than close friends.

It had been his ambition once to move to the country and adopt the manners and lifestyle of a country doctor and gentleman, but he had found, increasingly, in his visits to Oxfordshire, that the charms of rural life were quickly replaced, even after two or three days, by a sense of oppression into which the darkest of thoughts pursued him. Thus it was, on such occasions, that he sought refuge in the safe anonymity of the city from which, so recently, he had escaped.

"The black dog," he would sometimes say, "an ancient affliction, and there are many he pursues besides myself."

He was protected from his loneliness only by the habits which thirty years of professional life and a bachelor's existence had accrued around him, and after dinner, it was his settled habit to retire to his study and deal with any correspondence which had arisen from the day's business.

On this particular evening, he was keen to despatch the business which Harcourt had charged him with as quickly as possible. As he sat down to write, his pen poised over a fresh sheet of paper, he asked himself the question which, for thirty years, he had always asked himself before making any professional judgement that would have consequences for other people: do I believe myself to be right?

He was uncomfortable to be pronouncing a judgement about the girl without having seen her since August when her recovery had seemed very promising, and was ill at ease, too, with his own willingness to succumb to the pressure Harcourt had put on him, which might be deemed a personal weakness; but those factors were of no significance if, in doing what he was doing, he could establish, to his own satisfaction, that he was doing the right thing.

He spread Isobel Harcourt's letter to James Pennington on the table and read it again, very slowly, line by line. There was certainly evidence of strong and potentially destructive feelings there and a dangerous lack of self-knowledge. It had clearly been a mistake to send her to Wales, for if the gentle open spaces and lack of regular order of the Cotswolds could disorder vulnerable spirits, how much more potent for such ill effects the rugged and wild landscape of Wales?

He located once more the phrase which had arrested his attention on his first reading of the letter.

Worth more to me than life itself… gladly sacrifice all that I hold most dear…give myself to you body and soul…

A very distant memory came to him of having once, as a young man, made protestations of love as vehement as these, and one might argue that they fell within the provenance of fashionable romanticism, but did that make them any less dangerous, in certain circumstances, and perhaps especially in the case of a young woman?

For a moment the image of Laetitia Greville appeared to his inner vision, Letty, the object of his infatuation during a two-month period in the spring of a certain year. Her engagement to Charles Statham had put an abrupt end to that courtship, and he had in fact been glad, for the severance had made it possible for him to see the irrationality of his behaviour.

From then he had started to build his life on solid and rational foundations. There were certain values which had to be upheld for the good of society: rank and class being the framework which, together with a morality underpinned by religion and the law, formed the foundation. Marriage had its place, certainly, and to that, love also, for people are bound together by affection, as much as by property and custom, but uncontained love was like an uncontained storm, capable of infinite damage. Out of this orderly structure, people learn their duties and develop their proper codes of behaviour. It was in that framework that he had always conducted his business as a doctor and as a magistrate, and it was within that framework that he always asked himself the question, am I right, do I believe myself to be right?

He began his letter, *to whom it might concern, regarding the case of Isobel Harwood,* and, fortified by a small glass of brandy, set out the facts as plainly as plain language would render them. *A case suitable for discipline and correction, in sheltered circumstances,* he concluded, half an hour later, *for her own protection and future well-being.*

Was he right?

He drained the last drop of liquor from the glass.

Yes, he believed himself to be right.

He hurriedly sealed the letter, and summoned his coachman, Harry. "See this is delivered to Evesham Place, tonight."

Don't delay, he might have added, *lest I change my mind.*

Chapter 33

1635

Thou standest indicted in the name of Thomas Cheadle, late of Cheadle Moseley in the county of Cheshire, and of Beaumaris, not having the fear of God before your eyes, but being moved and seduced by the instigation of the devil, in the sixth year of the reign of our sovereign lord, Charles the first, by the grace of God, of England, Scotland, France, and Ireland, king, defender of the faith, feloniously, voluntarily, and with malice aforethought, did conspire with Anne, erstwhile Lady Anne Bulkeley, of Baron Hill, Beaumaris, by poison, to murder Sir Richard Bulkeley, late of Baron Hill Beaumaris. How sayest thou, Thomas Cheadle, art thou guilty of this murder whereof thou standest indicted, or not guilty?

Not guilty.

How wilt thou be tried?

By God and by my country.

God send thee a good deliverance. You gentlemen of the jury, look upon the prisoner, and hearken to his cause. He stands indicted by the name of Thomas Cheadle, as before in the indictment. Upon this indictment he has been arraigned, and thereunto has pleaded not guilty, and for his trial has put himself on God and his country, which country you are. Your charge is to enquire, whether he be guilty of the murder whereof he stands indicted, in manner and form as he stands indicted, or not guilty.

My lord, said the Prosecutor, it will appear to be a most barbarous act, to murder a man in this manner; for the man gave him no manner of provocation, and yet for motive, what greater motive do we require, than the desire which a man may conceive to possess that which belongs to another man…

And so it began.

Had I wished to kill him, I would have done it many years ago.

Lady Anne, will you describe for the court, the manner of your late husband's death?

His illness was an old infirmity, a sickness of the stomach which had troubled him from time to time for many years.

An old infirmity, you say. And did this old infirmity produce such excessive purging, such black vomit, such withering of the flesh as was reported by his physician?

His sickness increased in violence during the last days.

It is alleged, Mr Cheadle, that you procured a quantity of strong ratsbane in the period shortly before your employer's death.

I did. It was my business to procure all manner of things necessary for the house.

It is further alleged that your purpose in so doing was to administer a quantity sufficient to bring about the extreme illness and subsequent death to your master, Sir Richard. How say you?"

It is not so. The poison was acquired only for the purpose for which it was intended. I have witnesses who will confirm that at that particular time the problem with vermin at Baron Hill was extreme.

And for no other reason?

None. Is it likely that, supposing I had an evil intention against Sir Richard, that I would have procured the means to encompass it in so open a fashion, thereby throwing suspicion on myself? If you think so, you insult my intelligence or call your own into question.

It is alleged that poison was introduced to Sir Richard's tobacco, thereby procuring the means of his death. How say you to this?

I say it is nonsense. The tale was put out by his man, who was hysterical, believing himself to have been the unwitting cause of his master's death. Moreover, the body was inspected, not only by his physicians, but by the Bishop of Bangor, who confirmed that it was not an unnatural death. This verdict was upheld by the magistrate. Why am I called again?

Bring into the court Thomas Owen.

Bring in Thomas Owen.

Thomas Owen, what is your occupation?

I am a retained servant at Hen Blas in Beaumaris.

The home of Sir Richard's mother and brother?

Yes.

And what was your occupation at the time of Sir Richard's death?

I was a retained servant at Baron Hill.

And you knew the accused, Thomas Cheadle, as an employed man in your master's service?

He was his secretary.

And what do you have to tell this court?

Sir, it is common knowledge that he would lie with her, when the master was away.

Lie with her? The mistress?

Yes, sir. Lady Anne.

Thomas Cheadle looked towards Sir Rupert Lyme, the attorney from London whom he had engaged, at considerable expense, to take his case. So far he had been very quiet, seeming almost without interest at what was going on in the courtroom. Now, however, he rose.

Common knowledge? He asked.

Yes, sir.

And upon what evidence?

On the evidence of what was seen and heard.

And tell me, Thomas Owen, what was seen and heard by you in particular?

Not me in particular.

Not you in particular?

Well, sir...

Remember you are under oath.

No sir, not by me.

By whom, then? By whisperers? By gossips? By tittle-tattlers?

They may be something of that, sir, but…

By backstairs malingerers who will hear the creak of their own footsteps and swear it is an interloper, or the rustle of leaves and swear it the divestment of a petticoat? Or the rush of the wind about the eaves and swear it a deep-drawn sigh. Or the mew of a cat and I know not what else! Is it on such evidence as this that you would impugn the name of your mistress?"

The courtroom laughed. Thomas Owen was not a strong witness. There were others who could do Cheadle more damage, if they came forward.

"A man smokes a pipe of tobacco and dies clutching his stomach," said Sir Rupert, addressing the jury, "so what? There are a hundred different ways of dying a painful death that God has made for us, just as strange as that. Tears are shed, prayers are offered, the man is buried and that's that. A little later, the widow announces she is going to marry again, the man of her choice a former servant. Now the family pride is up like a dog's hackles, and now the dead man's brother says he was poisoned. On what evidence? There's rat's bane in the house. So is there in many a house. There's antimony in his closet, and a hundred other emetics and preparations, treatments and cordials that he put there himself. As his widow has testified, and no man has contradicted her, Sir Richard was no stranger to sickness. So, no case to answer. His wife, it is now alleged, has played the hobbyhorse. Still no case to answer, but people prick their ears up, and cry foul. Mud sticks. What better way of discrediting the widow and her new husband than by making of them the matter for skimmington rides and broadside ballads?"

Sir Rupert sat down and dabbed his brow with a kerchief, seeming once again to have lost all interest in the case, but he had had the effect he intended. The jurymen looked at one another as if to gauge each other's thoughts.

But the court was not done with him yet.

Is it true, Mr Cheadle, that in May of this year and again in June and July you visited London with the express design of using bribery and other illicit means to influence the outcome of this court. To hinder justice by corrupting the officers of the crown...

It was true. A man who sees a storm approaching seeks shelter. The world is not a perfect place, and justice is an instrument upon which powerful men can play with deft fingers, and his opponents were powerful men. But there were people with influence who had cause to be grateful to Thomas Cheadle; his word in a lawsuit over rents, his word in a dispute over land, his knowledge of harmful evidence that had been kept hidden long enough not to come to court. A man does not face the gallows without considering how best to use every card that has been dealt him in his hand.

My life was in question. I am a stranger in this country, and I had many adversaries whose power I greatly feared. I thought in the case of life and death, I might do it to protect myself against injury in the knowledge of my innocence and seeing no other course open to me.

Another day passed, another night. From his cell, Thomas Cheadle sent a note to Lady Anne, telling her to be of good cheer, though in truth he felt the case was slipping away.

The jurymen retired to consider their verdict.

The crowds inside the courthouse, the crowds that gathered outside each day to scavenge the morsels of gossip, all waited for the expected outcome, and there was not a man, a woman or a child in Beaumaris who did not relish the prospect of seeing Thomas Cheadle, and his lady with him, led away to the gallows.

On the charge of murder, how do you find the accused, Anne Cheadle?

Not guilty.

A murmur went round the courtroom. Thomas Cheadle caught Anne's eye and smiled; but her face was still white with anxiety. It had always been the likely case that he, and not she, would be convicted.

On the charge of murder, how do you find the accused, Thomas Cheadle?

Not guilty.

There was a moment of silence, and then a rumble of dissent. The judge had to bring the room to order, rapping his gavel with increasing vehemence.

Thomas Cheadle, you have found great mercy. Yet, this trial having made manifest your many attempts to pervert justice, that consort ill with the character of an innocent man, I do hereby order you to good behaviour and admonish you and your lady to go your way, and sin no more, lest worse befall you.

Chapter 34

London, October 1831

Mrs Bryant, Dr Fairhurst's housekeeper, was concerned about her employer's state of mind.

"He hasn't eaten a morsel for three days," she said to Harry, the doctor's coachman, who occasionally slipped into the kitchen for a cup of tea in the evening. "He pushes it around the plate, he arranges it this way and that way, so that whereas the beef started here and the cabbage there, the cabbage ends up here and the beef there, but, if I'm any judge, what's left at the end is just the same as what started out, and only fit to be sent next door for their dog Ruffles to chomp on which is a pity if you ask me, though I daresay the dog doesn't mind."

"If it's beef," said Harry, "you might think of sending it my way rather than Ruffle's way in future. You'll not find me as particular as the doctor, certainly not in respect of beef."

"I sometimes wonder if it's my cooking that is not to his liking, though he's never complained before in fifteen years. Fifteen years and never a complaint Harry, and now this."

"It'll not be your cooking, Mrs B, I can stand witness to that. If you need any testimonials about the high standard of your cooking, I'm your man."

"Perhaps he's sickening for something. Have you noticed anything, Harry?"

"Now you're asking!" said Harry. "I'll have to think about that one."

Thinking about things was not a skill Harry practised with any regularity, and his lack of proficiency in it was not something that lowered his self-esteem in any way. He was a man who liked to obey instructions, and in that sense, as he frequently admitted in convivial company, he would have been well suited to a career in the military, except that he did not very much like the idea of being wounded or killed, which was like to have proved a drawback.

He tried now to flex those muscles which controlled the thinking part of his anatomy, putting himself under a strain which was very obvious to Mrs B as she observed his facial contortions to a point where she felt obliged to pour him a third cup of tea.

It was true that the doctor had ordered him to drive the carriage to a remote part of the river on the Essex side, and had stood for a long time on a much decayed jetty contemplating the turbid water flowing beneath his feet; it was true that he had twice directed him to drive to Evesham Place and had then changed his mind and ordered him to drive straight back without leaving the carriage; it was true that recently he had been aware, in his driver's seat, of long drawn sighs and mutterings from within, almost as if the doctor were having a conversation with himself, but that, he put it to himself - now that he had his thinking cap on - could well be explained by the fact that the doctor wasn't eating properly, for a man who has not eaten for three days might well go about sighing to himself, or ordering strange journeys, or standing on the banks of swollen rivers for no apparent reason.

"No," said Harry, at last, "I can't say I've noticed anything."

Chapter 35

The black dog may roam around the grounds at will but so long as the doors are securely bolted, and the shutters firmly locked, he may not enter the house. So Septimus Fairhurst reasoned with himself in one of the several forms which his discourse regarding the old enemy took. The black dog may transmogrify into a thunder-laden sky, or into a thick and impenetrable fog, but so long as a man is prepared for the worst weather and has his compass about him, he may traverse the blackened or fog-bound moor and come safe to the other side.

In his recent dreams, however, there were no such comforting analogies; the dreams, properly speaking, contained no clear narrative, being more a matter of incoherent images and tumultuous feelings, but if he imagined himself wandering naked and blindfold through the mud of a formless heath, or returning home to find the doors and shutters of his house ripped asunder and prey to the invasion of any wandering beast, that would come somewhere near to explaining the terror he felt, and from which he awoke - with a sudden start and bathed in sweat - in the formlessness of the hour before dawn light.

Something had happened to destroy the tenuous and fragile balance in which certain obligations and understandings prevented the world from falling into chaos, and that thing was contained in the letter which he had sent to Evesham Place. Now, instead of the commonplace ennui or the oppressive feelings with which, it seemed, it was his daily business to contend, he felt the hollow and relentless chill of guilt.

Strong liquor, he had always found, taken in moderation, could provide a temporary anodyne to his affliction; now he found, with the bottle open beside him, the glamour of oblivion beckoning him onwards beyond moderation. Before oblivion, however, there were certain other stages which, like a series of plateaux, had to be crossed. The first was by no means unpleasant. Feelings of well-being, warm, almost like happiness, coursed through his veins, and had there been company present, he would have been able to enter, he felt, into the most affable vein of sociable conversation. In the next stage, as his head became lighter, long forgotten feelings and yearnings began to flood through him so that he wanted, simultaneously, both to laugh with joy and cry with pity. Letty, he cried aloud, Letty! It was as this stage reached its climax and began to wane, that he took pen and paper and began to write.

When, the next day, he awoke, with physical symptoms of malaise which temporarily occluded his spiritual malady, and with the paper still in front of him on the table, this is what he found.

Is it a sin to love? By heavens, I think not!

It is the devil who is the enemy of love, the eternal destroyer, always at his work.

Am I to be damned for another's wickedness? Is a life to be blighted at my instigation?

The black dog swells and the hungrier he is the greater he grows. I feel the fetid mist of his breath. Let me act now before he sinks his yellow fangs into my soul.

Beware the mountains and the open spaces, where your love roams for the devil will have her imprisoned between four black walls. None escape the madhouse. Those who are sane become mad there, and those who are mad are lost. There is no cure.

My God, said Dr Fairhurst, did I write this drivel! He screwed the sheet up, threw it into the last embers of the fire, and then took another sheet of paper. On this he wrote the following:

Mr Pennington, there is no time to lose. Harcourt is about to set out for Baron Hill, in Beaumaris, Wales. He intends to have his ward Isobel put away in a lunatic asylum. Unless you intervene to prevent his malice, this will be done.

He looked at the address on Isobel Harcourt's letter and transcribed it onto his own. Then he sealed it and called his coachman.

"Harry," he said. "Take this to Jennyfield Lane, number 17. Without delay."

Chapter 36

Beaumaris, October 11th, 1831

My dearest James

It is with some trepidation that I find excuses, as often as I may, to visit the Post Office in Beaumaris in the hope of receiving a letter from you, but so far in vain! But I do not despair! I know the post is unreliable, and, much as I love Emily, I cannot be certain that she is not under instructions from Mr Harcourt to intercept any letters that may arrive here for me. I know she has received letters from my guardian but she has said nothing to me of their content.

I think they both suspect that I am mad and need protection from myself. Emily worries about me quite unnecessarily, but there were certain incidents, when we first arrived here, to which her anxiety may be attributed.

On the second or third night, I awoke in the darkness, hearing noises. At first I thought it must be something I had dreamed, but then I heard it again, quite clearly in the room, the voice of a woman, a sound which seemed to indicate some kind of endurance or distress.

When, as I explained this, I heard the maids laughing, I realised that they had put some lewd construction on it and felt my face grow scarlet with embarrassment, but I am fairly sure that Emily, and Thomas, the man who looks after us here, drew the conclusion that I had imagined the entire episode.

A day or so later, we were sketching outside, and I included in my composition a woman and two little girls who had approached across the field whilst we were drawing. When

Emily saw my work, she questioned this, and pressed me to agree that it was of my imagining, though of course it wasn't. What I did not tell her was that a man had also walked across the meadow to meet them, and that when they met, one of the little girls threw herself towards him affectionately, to be twirled around. Indeed, had I not been already committed to drawing the woman and the children with their baskets of flowers, I might well have chosen the man and the child as the topic for my study.

Had this been purely a delusion, I am sure I would have felt some kind of discomposure, but I felt none. I felt vindicated in this, when, a few days later, I was looking out of the window towards the fields where, in the distance, some autumn bonfires were burning, and saw them again, just the man and the woman this time, walking so close together that one could well have imagined their hands firmly closed in each other's.

I called Emily, but by the time she had put down her needlework and come to the window, they had passed on..

"What?" she asked.

"Nothing. Just the smoke from the bonfires."

However, I know that Emily watches me and worries at the slightest thing, and so I have developed a way of anticipating her thoughts and humouring her!

I will not, in finishing this letter, indulge in fulsome sentiment. If you received my last, you will know my feelings, and I need not repeat them. If, as in my worst moments I fear, your own feelings have grown cold towards me, I will not blame you but will try to reconcile myself to a life of disappointment, knowing what happiness I had almost in my grasp.

I remain, always, your devoted friend.

Isobel Harcourt.

Chapter 37

"I'd like you to take me to the river again, Harry, " said Doctor Fairhurst.

"Very good, sir," said Harry, heartily, always happy to have an order to obey. "Same place as last time, sir?"

"Same place, Harry."

Within half an hour, the commotion of the city was left behind, and open fields stretched in front of them on each side.

"Very nice morning, sir," called Harry, who didn't particularly like the countryside but who felt that his master would appreciate a little cheerful conversation.

"Very nice, Harry."

"It's a tonic to the spirits, ain't it, sir?"

"A tonic, Harry. You express it perfectly."

Pleased with himself, Harry drove on. He didn't want to overburden his master with cheerful conversation, but he thought it might be in order to whistle a little, for he prided himself that he had a very tuneful whistle.

"Here we are, sir," he said at last. "This is the place, I think."

The old jetty was just a short distance away, looking even more rickety and decayed than Harry remembered it.

"Yes," said Doctor Fairhurst, "this is it?"

"Will you take a walk, sir?" said Harry.

"Yes, Harry. I think I will."

"Shall I wait here for you, sir?"

"Actually, Harry, I should like you to drive back to town."

"On my own, sir?"

"Yes, on your own."

"Is that an instruction, sir."

"Yes, Harry, an instruction."

"Very good, sir," said Harry, very glad that nothing was to be left to his discretion, for having to exercise discretion brought with it the uncomfortable business of having to think.

"And am I to come back for you later?" asked Harry.

"On the table in my study, Harry, there are some letters which I should like you to deliver to the addresses stipulated."

"Very good, sir."

"There is one letter for you, Harry. It will make your instructions very clear."

"Thank you, sir," said Harry, with genuine gratitude, for there was nothing he liked better than a very clear set of orders to obey.

He set off, turning just once to see Dr Fairhurst standing on the jetty. As he turned the corner, by a clump of trees, he began to whistle again, this time allowing himself the full range of trills and warbles from which he had respectfully refrained earlier.

By the time he was fully out of sight, the platform of the jetty was empty.

Chapter 38

London, October 1831

"I sometimes think," said James Pennington to his companion Kit one night in Cutler's Tavern, "that it would be a fine thing to blow my own brains out."

"An interesting proposition," said Kit, "the question is, is it a matter of purely philosophical speculation or a plan of action?"

"I have a pistol dedicated to the purpose."

"Very good. In that case it would be foolish of me to attempt to dissuade you. But just as a matter of idle curiosity, what, if I may, ask, has brought all this on?"

"What do you mean, what has brought it all on? Life has brought it on. What else?"

"Oh good, I'm relieved. I thought it might have been something I said."

"Don't jest with me you dog."

"Well, have another drink then, and reconsider."

So saying, he clicked his fingers and Marjorie, the tavern wench, came to replenish their glasses.

"Tell me," said Kit, having allowed sufficient time for Pennington's mood to change – usually not long. "when you disappeared for a day and a half with the beautiful Miss Harcourt all those months ago, "what exactly were you planning to do?"

"Elope."

"Marry?"

"Yes, you dog, that's what elope means, does it not?"

"And then what?"

Pennington shrugged his shoulders.

"Then perhaps Harcourt did you a favour, after all!"

"Do you know what angers me most, Kit?"

"Well, I might try to guess, but since I suspect you're going to tell me anyway, the best thing might be for me to stand aside and let you hold forth."

"Do you know what angers me most?" said Pennington, regardless. "I'll tell you what angers me most, that talentless, arrogant, spineless philistines like Harcourt, who loses more money in gambling dens in a week than I earn from my work in a year, who rides about in a coach from one salon to another all day, and lords it at banquets and balls and the opera and what have you not, that filthy undeserving rogues and charlatans such as him, can call themselves patrons of the arts, patrons of the arts, Kit!"

"So," said Kit when Pennington's whirlwind had finally blown itself out, "nothing new there then."

"Oh God," said Pennington. "I don't know why I don't just blow my brains out."

"Have another drink," said Kit, once again clicking his fingers. "Anyway, where's Meg? I've not seen her for three days."

"Don't ask me."

"Have you had a row with her again?"

"Well, she's impossible to work with."

"Are you sure it's not you who's impossible to work with?"

Pennington shrugged his shoulders.

"I don't know why you don't marry Meg. You're just like an old married couple sometimes."

"If I married Meg, it would be the end of me, and probably the end of her, too."

"You lie with her often enough for a wife."

"That's different."

"How?"

"It's an understanding. A working relationship."

"Like marriage. You make my point for me."

"What do you think of this?" said Pennington. "I'll paint her face in the second Isobel. That'll tickle her vanity enough to entice her back."

"So, you want to entice her back. Like I said, it's a marriage."

"No, like I said, it's business. I need her to dress up as a boy."

"Enlighten me. Lest I think you sinking further into depravity!"

"I've got a commission, didn't I tell you? The son of Lady Merton. She wants him rendered with dignity, nobility, gracefulness. It's hopeless. He's fifteen. He has no bearing. No concentration. He fidgets, he picks his nose, he scratches his bollocks, he slouches, he farts, he has the face of a piglet and the body of a slug.– how am I meant to achieve dignity, nobility, grace with that sort of material?"

"So that's where Meg comes in!"

"I need Meg to model the figure and then I can paint the sloucher's chops on it when I've done."

"What about the truth?"

"They don't want the truth. No-one wants the truth."

"Why don't you paint landscapes."

"There's no money in it."

"What about Constable?"

"Shall I tell you something about Constable? He's been painting for fifty years and he only ever sold twenty paintings in England. One day everyone will want Constable and by that time he'll be dead."

"Perhaps it'll be the same with you."

"Unless I choose to blow my brains out first."

"Ah, yes," said Kit, "there's always that."

Chapter 39

19th October 1831

This morning, we visited the town of Porthaethwy to look at the new bridge there which straddles the Menai Strait. We were driven there by Thomas in the landau and pair. In order to protect the aspect at the front of the house, the driveway runs to the rear, with the wooded slopes above, though architecturally this is where the front portico of the house is, and it was here the carriage was waiting for us, as arranged, at ten o'clock. In one direction, the driveway goes towards the small villages of Llanfaes and Llangoed, where, we are told, there is a church at which the family worships, and where some of their ancestors lie buried; in the other it makes a slow progress through the woodland, then down the hill to the great iron gates and lodge a quarter of a mile from Gallows Point. Not far from the house – a distance of two or three hundred yards - the track crosses a bridge over the public road from Beaumaris to Llansadryn and Pentraeth, known as Allt Goch Fawr, and just here there is a small gatehouse which, as Thomas informed us, is known as the hunting lodge, though he could adduce no reason for this other than that this is what the servants have always called it.

    The drive from there is pleasant enough, emerging from the woodland to become a tree lined avenue with farmland on each side, as it descends towards the coast road.

    This road, running from Beaumaris to Porthaethwy, was constructed some twenty-five years ago by the Lord Bulkeley of that time, to facilitate travel between the two towns. Before that, communication between the two was only possible using tedious and circuitous inland routes. Before the coastal road was built, the natural coastline comprised wooded slopes descending steeply from the high summit of the hill above all the way to the rocky water's edge.

The rest of the journey to Porthaethwy is very pretty. The road turns and curves to afford a variety of scenic prospects, through the trees – now with their autumn leaves – across the water to the further shore, rocky inlets, and creeks which carry the water courses debouching from the hillside. On each side of the road, here and there, are pretty whitewashed cottages, some built tightly up against the slope, some perched on the rocks above the water.

Porthaethwy, as Thomas informed us, has grown considerably since the beginning of the construction of the bridge, which was completed five years ago, and now a steady stream of carriages and farm wagons, and herds of sheep, pigs and cattle flow across to the island and from the island to the mainland shore at a point which stands a mile distant from the city of Bangor.

The bridge itself is a marvel of engineering. To view it from a distance is to see a construction not only of great magnificence but of great beauty. To see it from the shore, just below, is to experience the mightiness of the achievement, for the towers and arches are built on the solid rock that emerges from the swirling flood when the tide is low, and the great iron chains with which the central roadway is suspended, were hoisted into place by hundreds of men, a feat witnessed by many more, all expecting, as Thomas told us, disaster to befall the enterprise at any moment.

We took refreshment in a private room at an inn near the bridge on the Anglesey side, and returned in the middle of the afternoon, passing the hunting lodge at about four o'clock; when pressed, Thomas informed us that the lodge is sometimes inhabited by a gardener and his family, though at present it is unoccupied. It was built, he thinks, as a gatehouse guarding the private drive from the road below, at the time the bridge across the road was built but it may be that at some time, hunting parties, on horseback or on foot, used it as a meeting point where the men took refreshment and the hounds water.

We are inclined to think more highly of Thomas than hitherto. Our first impression was of someone of a surly and disposition, but now we see that his is simply a quiet and serious temperament. He doesn't really mix in with the frivolous chit-chat and banter of the other servants. Amongst other things, he tells us, he is fond of reading the poetry of Wordsworth and Shelley. Certainly, he is very courteous towards us, and solicitous of our needs and wishes.

22nd October 1831

In one night, the season has changed. Yesterday all was mellow gold and rich scarlet; in the night, the wind thrashed so that the trees are reduced to skeletal forms with the cold daylight filtering through their naked branches.

Yesterday we were taken to see the earthworks at Aberlleiniog which some people call a castle though I don't believe it is one in any true sense of the word. There are two ways of reaching this landmark. One is to take the coastal road towards Penmon, as far as the hamlet of Lleiniog, and thence to follow a short uphill track through farmland. The other – and the one we took – involves a somewhat longer walk, starting from the village of Llangoed, and following the course of a small stream which runs down the hill, broadening after quarter of a mile where another stream joins it.

The woodland here is quite dense, and the path, infrequently used in these latter days, is somewhat uneven, muddy and overgrown in places, and the wayside is strewn with fallen leaves. When we had walked a mile, the outline of the earthworks came into view high above us through the trees, and because, as Thomas explained, the approach follows a track which winds first this way and then the other through the vegetation, and because my boot was already rubbing sorely, I announced that I would walk no further, save to return to the carriage. I said to Isobel that she might go on, if she wished, with Thomas to show her the way, but I rather hoped she would decline this offer. This she did not, and as a result I found myself waiting alone for more than forty minutes until they returned. Then, much to my annoyance, Isobel, flushed with her adventure, proceeded to fill the remainder of our walk back to the landau with a detailed account of how they had scrambled up the thorn strewn goat track up to the summit of the mound, and of the splendour of the view from this vantage point. Suffice it to say that by the time we reached home, I was thoroughly out of sorts and wished only to be left alone to my own company.

She is my dearest sister, and I love her without reserve, but I do sometimes think that Isobel is so accustomed, through her misadventures, to being the centre of attention, that she sometimes scarcely allows, certainly as far as I am concerned, that other people have their own independent existence, and feelings of their own towards which some consideration is due!

Chapter 40

London, October 1831

"Remarkable," said Kit.

"What?" said Meg, with the abruptness of one expecting mockery.

"Astonishing," said Kit.

"What?" repeated Meg.

She was standing in the pose which James Pennington had instructed her to adopt, wearing a dark blue frock coat, breeches and stockings, a waistcoat, shirt and cravat, and with her hair taken back from her face to a tail which protruded from underneath the back of a tricorn hat.

"What do you think, then?" said Pennington, who had told Kit to call in on his way to Cutler's to enjoy the treat of seeing Meg in the pose of a well-bred youth.

"She has the pertness of a boy, and yet it is a pertness no boy could ever achieve."

"What are you talking about?"

"She has the arrogance of a boy..."

"Doesn't she just!" said Pennington.

"She is the perfect boy and yet no boy could ever be so perfect."

"Do the voice, Meg," said Pennington, pleased that Kit was suitably impressed.

Meg felt her face colouring, but it was partly with pleasure. "I say, Pontefract, have a care!" she began. "Damn me if it isn't time for Tiffin. Do me the honour of taking a turn with me on the Serpentine, old boy!"

"Excellent!" said Kit, roaring with laughter.

"Now keep still," said Pennington when the laughter had

subsided, "I haven't finished working yet."

"What did you ask him here for?" asked Meg, when Kit had continued with his evening walk to Cutler's.

"I wanted him to see what a handsome boy you make."

"Well, it would be a bad look out for me if I didn't."

Pennington thought for a moment. "No, it's not quite the same thing."

"Would you fancy me if I was a boy, then? That's a bit queer isn't it?"

He stared at her thoughtfully. "No," he said, at last. "If I disrobed you and discovered you actually were a boy, I'd be disgusted. It's something else. Something to do with the intrigue of illusion. There's something fascinating about disguise. Keep still!"

"I am keeping still!"

"In Twelfth Night, for example," he continued, "which I wouldn't expect you to know or even to have heard of, but which is a play by William Shakespeare, Viola wears her twin brother's clothes, and Olivia falls in love with her thinking she's a boy. Well, of course, in the original theatre, Viola would have been acted by a boy, anyway, but then, you see, so would Olivia. So, you see there's a kind of provocative illusion about it all."

"It sounds a bit queer to me."

"It's all in appearances. That's what's intriguing about the world. Everything appears to be what it is not. Behind every deception there is an illusion. Right, that'll do for tonight."

"Can I take this lot off now?"

"Yes but do it slowly so that I can enjoy the layers of illusion being peeled away."

"You want me to strip, is that it?"

"Don't be coarse, Meg. You know how much I hate coarseness. But, yes, if you like, but very, very slowly, mind you. In "Measure for Measure," which is another play, Isabella dresses as a nun, then when she reveals herself to the Duke, her massed curls tumble down in a golden cascade. Remarkable."

"You're not dressing me up as a nun," said Meg, decisively. "It'd have my grandmother turning in her grave!"

Chapter 41

1645

"*Sir* Thomas Cheadle! What's this?" asked Cheadle.

His son, Richard, continued to read: "In respect of loyal and valiant service in securing the stronghold and defences at Beaumaris, and at Aberlleiniog, conferred by his Majesty, King Charles, in Oxford, this seventh day of April 1645... Thomas Cheadle, Knight of the Realm. Sir Thomas."

"Ha!" snorted Cheadle, in brusque mirth. "They love me, now, do they?"

"Congratulations, father!"

"What nonsense. It's not long since they would have had my neck in a rope. Still would if they could. Your former brother-in-law and his hot-head of a son."

"The king knows your worth," said his wife, Anne. "That means that there are people who speak on your behalf. Important people."

"This means that you are a *Ladyship*, now, mother!" said Richard, with high pleasure. Lady Anne, or Lady Cheadle. I think Lady Anne sounds more courtly, don't you?"

Cheadle and his wife exchanged a glance; the title *Lady Anne* carried an old familiar resonance: a young mother, with three children and a titled husband.

What struck Cheadle most, however, was how easily his son, Richard, had come to use the term *mother*. He had never known his own mother, of course, and had carried no bitterness of feeling towards Anne when he had been brought to Anglesey, nearly a year ago, but still it pleased his father that a term used at first with simple politeness, had now taken on a homely warmth of natural affection.

"I think I would prefer to be Lady Cheadle. It conveys more of the redoubtable old lady, don't you think?"

"You're not an old lady!" said Richard. "At least, I don't think so. And I know my father doesn't think so!" he added with a bubble of slightly ribald laughter.

There were some who said that she had disowned her own children after the death of her first husband, Sir Richard, and her second marriage.

It was not so.

Both daughters were married to families of standing, Ann to Henry Whyte of Fryars, and Mary to Richard of Bodychen. It did not do for them, however, to have open social intercourse with a woman who had stood trial for murder and who was reputed to have been an adulteress when their father was alive. The meetings between them had become formal, brief, courteous, such affection as there was constrained to politeness. They had their husbands and their connections to think of.

Anne had remained strong, never wavering. Had she dissociated herself from him, then, when she first became a widow, she could have spared herself a great deal of pain and opprobrium, but she had chosen without hesitation, to become his wife. Had she severed all ties with him, she would still be Lady Anne Bulkeley, of Baron Hill, at the centre of the family, and its wide circles of social influence, but instead she had chosen him. They had chosen each other.

The restoration of the outer walls at Aberlleiniog had been completed long before the rumours of war had made the refurbishment of Beaumaris a priority, but it had been conceded, even by his enemies, [though there were those who thought he was indulging in power politics] that a second defensive position, particularly on the exposed coast facing the Conway estuary, Ynys Seiriol and the northern approaches should be maintained.

"If it had been up to me," said Sir Thomas Bulkeley, Lady Anne's former brother-in-law, so close to Thomas Cheadle's face that his eyeball seemed to bulge with hatred, "I would have it ripped down, stone by stone, and leave it for the proper goats, not those who walk on two legs…"

But it was not up to him.

Masons had been commissioned to remake the four turrets to their full height and strength, looking out to sea, or down into the inner keep where the house, which Thomas Cheadle had envisaged as a young man, was now the home of the Cheadle family. It was on a scale much smaller than Baron Hill, but it had solid, square rooms, with leaded windows, and stone fireplaces and galleries with carved panels and a broad curving staircase.

She had always remained strong, but sometimes, when he came upon her alone, at a window looking out towards the sea, or sitting at her embroidery, the quick needle momentarily still, there was a look of abstraction on her face, as if looking into a place where no-one else could see.

"Nothing," she would reply when asked.

The trial, hanging over them for so long before, had taken its toll, he suspected, had sapped some of her inner spirit. A woman is more vulnerable to these things than a man.

It pleased him that his son had taken so warmly to her, however, for that had restored some of her spirit, and the boy's mirth seemed to have rekindled hers.

"He's a good boy," she said. "Your father did a good job with him. You should be proud of him."

It was true.

He was an able horseman, agile with the sword, though lacking the strength a man would need in battle, and perhaps some of the steel. He had inherited a large measure of his mother's mild nature. Though he had not seen her alive these twenty years, Thomas Cheadle fancied he could still see Sarah in the boy's eyes. He had thought once, almost still a boy himself, that he loved her, but it seemed distant now, as flimsy and unsubstantial as a dream, a breath on a mirror.

It was Anne, another man's wife, who had become the passion of his life. And there was tenderness between them yet, sometimes fire, even now. It was Anne who had taken his soul, and it was Anne with whom he would spend eternity, perhaps an eternity confined in hell.

Chapter 42

The kerfuffle at number 17 Jennyfield Lane had been going on, some people said, since ten o'clock in the morning; that, according to Margery Langton, the tanner's wife, who was hanging out washing in the yard below at the time, was when the first bit of nonsense had been thrown out of the window above on the third floor. The bit of nonsense in question was a painting and she called it a bit of nonsense because that was exactly what she believed it to be, and she had the same opinion of all paintings, not just those of James Pennington, though because she knew James Pennington personally, and had the lowest possible opinion of his loose morals and character, his paintings, she tended to think, were especially nonsensical.

By eleven o'clock, several pieces of similar nonsense had followed the first, enough, some people said, to light a sizeable bonfire, which, by twelve o'clock was exactly what had happened, producing plumes of black smoke which played havoc with Marjory Langton's white washing, so much so that she sent word to Mr Langton, the tanner himself, asking what he proposed to do about it. When word came back from the tannery that he proposed to do nothing about it but advising her that she might consider taking the washing down if she cared to, she went to bring the neighbours so that they could testify, if at any later stage testimony should be required, that her white wash had been pretty much ruined and would have to be done again.

Considerable outrage was now expressed, for the dirty smoky oily stains on Mrs Langton's white wash seemed to carry distinct moral overtones, and the flames themselves to have connotations of another fiery place where the creator of such nonsense was like soon to find himself. When the defiled washing had at last been taken in, however, and when the initial wildness of the fire had settled to a steady glow, there were several who took the opportunity to bring a kettle of water, or a pot of soup to be warmed up over the glow. Over the next hour, in addition, no less than five potatoes were very nicely baked for the sustenance of those who kept vigil to see what other nonsense might yet emerge from the third floor window above, or indeed, anything that might profitably be taken away to be sold, or, failing that, for use at home.

At four o'clock in the afternoon, a further hail of nonsense began to rain down, and the observers had to take cover inside Mrs Langton's back door, but when the storm abated, the dwindling fire was restocked, and in the fading light, it became the centre of a gathering more convivial than Jennyfield Lane had seen for many a year.

A shower of rain, however, soon put an end to that, and as the gathering dispersed, the fire began to hiss and spurt under the downpour, sending up new plumes of steam and dirty smoke.

It was the smoke which first alerted Meg Liddle that something was amiss. She was hurrying towards Cutler's, feeling, after a full day alone at home, the need for some cheerful company, when the dark smudge, beyond the rooftops on the far side of Vinegar Gardens came into view. It could have been a chimney on fire, it could have been the furnace at the tannery burning late, or any one of a dozen other sources that added their darkness to the darkening London sky, but something told Meg Liddle that this was coming from Jennyfield Lane.

When she reached the top of the stairs and entered the room, the sight that met her eyes was that of James Pennington, sitting on the bed, with his eyes closed, pointing a small silver pistol at his own head.

How long she stood there she could not afterwards recall. It seemed that time stood still, and she was dumbstruck, frozen to the spot. At some point, however, she realised that the expected explosion had not yet happened, and that James Pennington's frozen state was possibly of much longer duration than her own.

"What on earth are you doing!" she called, in a voice that came out as a high-pitched whimper.

"I can't do it," said Pennington, in a voice even more pitiful. "I can't do it."

"Give that to me," she said, now taking control of the situation.

Pennington's head dropped into his hands.

She put the pistol discreetly away in her bag and looked round the room.

"What have you done with all your..."

"Worthless!" said Pennington. "Worthless rubbish, the lot of it."

Catching her glance, he nodded towards the window.

"The fire," she said, "that was you!"

"Worthless," he repeated.

She sat down and took full count of the room's emptiness. It was a forlorn sight. Of the dozens of paintings, only three remained. The rest, and the cluttered, jumbled chaos of stacked frames and canvases, the tables covered with brushes and quills, palettes and mixing bowls, the scrolls and drawing books were all gone, leaving a pitiful remnant of odds and ends, scattered across the floor.

"What brought all this on?" she asked, at last.

"Nothing brought it on," said Pennington, his head still in his hands.

"Why did you keep these?"

He looked up slowly, taking in the three remaining paintings, though with unseeing eyes.

They were going to go last."

"Don't destroy them," she said, going to kneel at his side. "You can begin again."

He looked at her and then at the room again. "My God," he said suddenly, as if something had clicked back into place, "what a mess!"

"Never mind," she said, "you can start again."

He shook his head. "I'm finished," he said, "finished."

"What..." She was about to reformulate her first question, when he opened his clenched fist to reveal a crumpled sheet of paper.

"What's that?"

He moved his hand beckoning her to take it. Carefully, she opened it, spreading it flat, and smoothing it with her fingers to remove the creases. She read the three lines of the message and then the signature, *Septimus Fairhurst.*

"There," he said. "Am I fit to live?"

"But this is not of your making."

"My cowardice, don't you see? My snivelling, spineless, gutless..."

As he paused to dredge up more words of self-abasement, Meg reflected on her own undisclosed role in this sequence of events, and seemed to hear the sound, distant and faint, but audible nonetheless of restlessness within a certain confined space in Lowfield Cemetery.

"I didn't even have the courage to..." he raised his hand to his temple in the motion of squeezing a trigger.

"Stop talking about that," she said. "It's over now, and you're not going to think about it anymore."

"I need a drink," he said, suddenly.

"Come on, I'll take you to Cutlers."

He stood up and then immediately sat down again. "No," he said. "I can't go there. I can't face Kit. Not tonight."

"Have you got anything here?"

He thought for a moment, with furrowed brow, and then pointed to a cabinet at the foot of the bed.

"What is it?" she asked, a moment later, screwing her face up at the taste.

"Rum."

"It's fiery!"

Gradually he became calm.

"When did it come, the message?"

"This morning."

"And is that why…"

He nodded his head.

"Do you believe it?" she asked.

"Why shouldn't I?"

"Can he do it? Have her put away, like that?"

"He can do anything he likes. That's money. There's no justice without money, no law. Money makes up all the rules. It's like ivy on a building."

"And she's a woman."

"What?"

"She's a woman."

"Yes. She's a woman."

He poured another tot into the two small glasses, and they sat for several minutes in silence.

"You've got to go and stop it," she said, suddenly.

"What!"

"You've got to go."

"But I can't do anything like that!"

"You have to. There's no-one else. Where is it?"

"Beaumaris. Somewhere in Wales."

"Do you know where?"

"Vaguely."

"Right. You'd better get some sleep. Catch the morning coach. No more of this."

"Just one last tot."

"Just one, then."

"God," he said. "All that work gone up in smoke, just think." And at that he began to laugh. Just a giggle at first, a little tricklet of escaping mirth, then a snort, then a full-blown gale.

When it had died down at last, she went to get her cloak. "I'll call by in the morning," she said, "See you get off all right."

"Can't you stay here with me tonight, Meg. One last night. You never know when you might see me again."

"I'll see you in the morning," she said, firmly. "And now you, get yourself into bed."

Meekly, he obeyed, and ten minutes later, she was making her way past the blackened wall of Deacon's Gate, not on her direct route home, but on her route by way of Lowfield cemetery.

Lowfield cemetery was not a place to which Meg Liddle would normally choose to go, even during the day, let alone at night. The fact that it was hallowed ground made little difference to her sense that the place was inhabited by ghosts, but whereas during the day, as she imagined, such ghosts as were loitering with evil intent would be pale and indistinct, at night, she conjectured, the ghosts might be clustered in the bushes, swarming like bees in the lower branches of the yew trees, or thronging the air unseen. The fact that the remnants of a river fog had crept up the hill to hover about the place during the night hours did not add any comfort to the prospect which met her as she passed through the old, rusted gates, which were always left open as if to provide a welcome to anyone who chose to enter, at any time of day, whether for the shorter or the longer stay.

Nevertheless, drawing her cloak around her, she made her way along the well-kept main path, and then along the lesser unmade paths which branched off from it, and then along the even lesser paths, overgrown with weeds, which led off from them until at last she came to the one small plot which was her destination.

Here, she kneeled, cleared away some of the larger weeds which had flourished since her last visit, and eventually, after checking over each shoulder in turn for any supernatural companionship, began to speak. "You probably know already why I'm here, gran, and I'm sorry if you've had more turns around down there than you've cared for in the time since I was here last, but I hope you'll see that I've tried to do some good for once, even though I love him more than she does, and even though it's not fair that just because she's a lady he can't see what's best for him, but even me, spiteful as I am, can see that it's not right for a person to be put away in a mad house without cause, and if I could have kept him here I would, but I couldn't as he is probably the only hope she has of avoiding a terrible fate. So that's why I've come here in the dead of night and almost wishing I hadn't, so shivering am I and so frightened of wandering ghosts, so that I could make sure you knew and could perhaps have a peaceful night for once. So, goodnight, gran, I'd better be away if I'm to see him off in the morning, for he's no doubt had another couple of tots since I come away, and he'll be wanting to lie abed, if I don't see to him."

With that, she stood, and after a hurried look about herself on each side, she scurried away towards the cemetery gates, fortified with a sense, notwithstanding her imaginings of pursuit by a host of otherworldly beings, that her grandma, for once, was deeply at rest.

Chapter 43

Meg was right in supposing that Pennington would take one or two more tots before finally abandoning himself to sleep. Where her prediction was incorrect was in her supposing that he would stop there, instead of going on to finish the entire bottle, which in fact is what he did.

By that time, a considerable amount of courage was coursing through his veins, and he saw himself carrying out brave deeds and winning the day. He would take on Harcourt, he would rescue Isobel, and love would triumph. They would travel abroad together, as planned before; he would paint the Alps, the countryside of Provence, the canals of Venice. He would be recognised and feted by the wealthy men of Europe, even though he disdained their riches. He would be a champion of liberty and reform.

It was a different story in the morning. When the first grey light of dawn seeped through the shutters, his body was so preoccupied with its own malaise that he hardly noticed it. When he opened his eyes at last, he took in the sight of the devastated studio. "My God," he said to himself, "what have I done! What have I done!"

He went to the window and peered down. There, three floors below, was the ashen heap that was all that remained of nearly ten years' work. He flung himself back on the bed, where other memories of the previous evening now began to filter back. Meg was here, he recalled, and we had a glass of rum, and then she said… Suddenly the whole thing came back to him, and a spasm of deep anxiety thrilled in his bowels.

A man who is truly alone with himself is capable of knowing

his own limitations, and at this moment in time, James Pennington knew his. As in the King's Head at Dartford, a complete lucidity came to him.

"This is simply something I cannot do."

All tropes of thought led back to this hard reality.

"If I were to go," he said at last, another trope suggesting itself, "if I were to go I would probably do more harm than good."

Pleased that this variation provided a morsel, however tiny, of exculpation, he decided to get up and get himself well out of the way before Meg arrived. He would lie low at Kit's for a couple of days and pick up the pieces from there.

The sound of feet on the stairs, however, feet that were all too recognisable, told him that it was already too late for this.

Part 3

Chapter 44

23rd October 1831

Mr Pennington is in the town. My guardian, who arrived here this morning, brought the news with him, and I am under strict instructions to protect Isobel from all knowledge of it. My first inclination was to suggest that we should all leave together, under my guardian's protection, but he was adamant that such a course of action would not be wise. If he will go to this extreme to follow her, he explained, he will stop at nothing. Some other means must be found to counter his menace.

24th October 1831

I am writing this now with the calmness of retrospection, but oh what a terrible hour had to be endured this morning when it was discovered that Isobel was missing. It was in the period just after breakfast, and the house was particularly busy in preparation for Lord Bulkeley's return in less than a week's time. When Isobel left the dining room, I assumed she had returned to her chamber, as is often her custom after breakfast, and I was glad of the opportunity to speak to my guardian alone further to discuss the situation we find ourselves in.

When I knocked on Isobel's door a short time after this, and got no reply, I immediately set out to look for her in other locations in the house where I thought she might be. I managed for some time to contain my panic, feeling sure that I would come across her at any moment, but when I had checked every corner of the house, I was forced to tell my guardian that she was not there, and though I tried to be calm when I heard my own voice it was fraught with alarm.

Together with Daniel, my guardian's valet, we searched the house again, and having confirmed my own suspicions, we went outside to search the grounds. I immediately went to the steps above the formal gardens but the prospect below was empty. Mr Harcourt and Daniel ran to the rear of the house to check the driveways on each side, and finding nothing there, decided to extend the search to the village. To this end, they went into the house to put on top coats and I followed them, saying that I would go with them, but my uncle would have none of this.

"Stay here," he said. "You can be of no assistance and may prove a hindrance."

"Don't worry," said Daniel, as Mr Harcourt strode off, "we'll find her. She can't have gone far."

This did little to reassure me, because I have known – as he has not - my sister's determination in these things heretofore, but I appreciated the kindliness of his intentions in contrast to my guardian's abruptness, and smiled at him, albeit a little wanly, to signify this.

When they had gone, I returned to the steps above the terrace, close to the place where we set up our easels, shortly after arriving here, where Isobel did her strange sketch, and then wandered slowly down towards the kitchen gardens, which occupy an extensive area, enclosed by high brick walls, to one side of the house. Here there are all kinds of outbuildings and glasshouses, together with vegetable and herb beds, and trellises for peas and beans, though at this season much of the main growth has gone, and there is something of a forlorn aspect to the place.

I was lost in thought, reflecting on the transient and melancholy nature of all things *sub specie aeternae*, which at least provided some soothing remission from my immediate anxiety about Isobel, when I heard a sound of laughter, so light and carefree that I wondered for a moment if I might be in danger of coming across one of the maids of the house in some secretive dalliance, or if I had succumbed to Isobel's weakness of hearing ghostly voices, before realising that the voice I heard was neither maid nor ghost, but, indeed, Isobel's own voice.

I made my way in the direction from which it seemed to come, and, turning past a summerhouse which still seemed full of greenery, I came across Isobel, sitting on the ground with two or three tiny kittens running over her lap and shoulders, and, on his haunches close by, Thomas.

"Emily!" she called, "look! Aren't they lovely. Aren't they absolutely beautiful!"

My intense relief contended with a sense of her irresponsibility, that she would go off, even here, without telling anyone, but then I remembered that neither she nor Thomas was aware of the presence of Mr Pennington in the town, and the strain which this has put upon those of us who do know it.

"She littered here, in the bushes. Look she made a place for herself, just like a nest. Thomas found her. She wouldn't let anyone else near, would she?"

"She was nearly wild," Thomas said, aware, I think of my disapproval. "That's the way they are with their young."

"She came out for Thomas," said Isobel, and then the kittens came out for me. And she doesn't mind at all. Look, she's quite content. It's giving her a bit of a rest, I think. Here, you take one, Emily, they're so beautiful. Just look at his face!"

In spite of myself, I took hold of the soft bundle which she held towards me and could not help but be charmed by the almost weightless form and the tiny whiskers and kitten features.

"Nature makes them like that," said Thomas, reading my thoughts.

"We'd better go back to the house," I said. "Mr Harcourt is concerned about you."

"But why?"

"We didn't know where you were."

"But I'm only here, not thirty yards from the house."

"Even so."

"But I'm with Thomas. What possible harm could I come to?"

"None, I'm sure," I said, not wishing to pursue the matter

further in the presence of a servant.

In the privacy of the house, however, I made no secret of my annoyance at the trouble she had caused. "Mr Harcourt and his man, Daniel, have gone into the town to look for you."

"But whatever for? Why in the name of reason and common sense would I go alone into the town without telling anyone?"

"You seem to forget, Isobel, your behaviour has not always been consistent with reason and common sense."

"If it is Mr Pennington you are referring to, and I suppose it must be, let me make it absolutely clear that I no longer harbour the slightest..." here she paused for a moment, "the slightest desire to see him, or hear from him, or have any knowledge of his business."

"Do you deny that you have written to him during the time we have been here in Beaumaris?"

"No, I don't deny it," she said, turning away towards the window.

I waited for her to continue.

"I wrote to him," she went on, at last. "There was so much unfinished business. So much I didn't understand. He didn't reply."

"And you have written to him only once?"

"I wrote a second letter, " she confessed. "I was going to get Thomas to take it to the post for me, but I changed my mind." At this, she turned and shrugged her shoulders. "I no longer think of him. It is finished. I have to live my life."

I did not allow myself to express the satisfaction this gave me but merely nodded.

"I'm going to my room," she said. "If Mr Harcourt wants to speak to me, that's where I'll be."

At the door, she turned. "Tell me Emily, what is your opinion of Mr Harcourt's valet?"

"Of Daniel? He seems a very pleasant young man."

"Pleasant, yes," she said.

"Why do you ask?"

"Oh, I don't know. I just wondered if you thought there was

anything strange about him."

"Strange? No. No, I don't think so," I replied, though for no reason which I could account for, I felt a slight flush come to my cheeks.

"It's not important," said Isobel, with a smile, as she turned to go."

I did not dwell on this but made my way to the avenue to await Mr Harcourt's return.

It was some twenty minutes before he appeared, and as I ran towards him to break my news, it was clear that he was alone.

"It's all right. She's here. She was in the garden. Thomas had taken her to show her something there."

"The world's gone mad," he said, with some exasperation, striding ahead of me so that I had almost to run to keep up with him.

"Where is Daniel?" I asked when he was taking off his top coat in the vestibule.

He did not answer until we were in the drawing room. "We went as far as the church, and I caught sight of Pennington on the corner. He hadn't seen us, but as soon as I pointed him out to Daniel, the scoundrel disappeared. One moment he was there, the next time I turned to him he was gone. Anyway, I followed Pennington at a distance, and it didn't take long for me to realise that wherever Isobel was, she wasn't with him. So, I came back."

I began my tale of what Isobel had confided in me with regard to James Pennington, hoping that this would help to put him in a happier frame of mind, but I had hardly started when Daniel appeared.

"Where the devil have you been!" said Mr Harcourt. "I don't pay you to disappear at the slightest whim. What have you got to say for yourself?"

For a moment, the young man – I say man, though he is scarcely more than a boy – seemed baffled and embarrassed, and whatever his misdemeanour, my heart went out to him.

"Well?" Mr Harcourt insisted.

"It was when you pointed him out…"

"Pennington?"

"Yes."

"Why, do you know him? Have you seen him before?"

"No, that's just it. I just thought…he could have turned to see you at any moment, and if he'd seen me…"

"Why should that make any difference?"

"My thought was simple. It may be that you will need me to do things, to ask questions, to find things out. How much easier is that if I am not known to him as being with you?"

Mr Harcourt considered this for a moment, nodded in a detached way, and then turned back to me.

I continued my account of Isobel's renunciation of James Pennington, but before I could complete it, he was already shaking his head.

"She may well say such things. To put us off the scent. This whole business of going into the garden with Thomas may well have been just such a subterfuge."

I recalled the circumstances in which I had come across Isobel with Thomas in the corner of the garden, the tiny kittens in her lap and running over her arms and her shoulders, and though I did not venture to say so, there was nothing about it, angry though I had been at that moment, that seemed in any way contrived or disingenuous.

"She has deceived us all once," Mr Harcourt continued. "She may well do it again. I fear that she may have been released from medical supervision too soon, and for this laxness, I feel deeply responsible. However, we must stay the time. His Lordship will be here within a week and we must not repay his hospitality with a family dispute. In the meantime, we must keep a strict watch on Isobel; but yet be gentle as if all is normal. Remember, she doesn't know that we know Pennington is here. And, yes, Daniel, you may well be right that there is a role for you in this. I'll give it some careful thought."

With this he went out of the room. I smiled at Daniel, as if to say that we had both played our part, but at the awkwardness of his own reaction, and the sudden flush which again came unbidden to my cheeks, I rather wished that I had maintained a more detached and formal attitude.

Chapter 45

1648

The men and horses had been gathering on Beaumaris Green day after day for a week. Men, horses, banners and flags, swords and lances, drums and hunting horns, a colourful array to stir the heart and fire the spirit with courage. The muster had grown each day, as the gentry of the island answered the call, bringing their men, who were hurriedly drilled and trained by the professional sergeants who had served at Naseby and Chester, and knew the strategies and counter strategies of modern warfare.

Sir Thomas Bulkeley, recently made Viscount Bulkeley of Cashel, and High Constable of Beaumaris, and his son, now Colonel Richard Bulkeley, were amongst those who rode by in their colours, exhorting the troops. Sir Thomas Cheadle and his son, Richard, approaching from Llanfaes, viewed the scene from the corner of the Green at Fryars Road.

"How can we be defeated with such numbers?" said Richard, thrilling at the sights and sounds that met them. "It's glorious."

Beaumaris had surrendered once, in 1646, after the fall of Chester, without a blow being struck, General Mytton riding into the town with a small group of men and offering honourable conditions of submission, which, under the threat of further action, had been accepted. The arrest and captivity of the king, however, had provoked insurrection and revolt through the length and breadth of Wales, and nowhere more passionately than on Anglesey.

"This is madness," said Sir Thomas Cheadle, drawing his horse alongside Captain Sanders, commander of the town's company.

"Don't let the men hear you say that!"

"You've read the declaration, haven't you, Cheadle?" called Lord Bulkeley.

"Aye, I've read it, and I know who drew it up."

"If you have traitorous designs, declare them now, once and for all. Then we'll all know what we've long suspected."

"When these men lie cold in their own blood," said Cheadle, directing his words to the Captain, "then let you remind their widows and orphans what was said."

"They are loyal subjects, Thomas. They fight for their king."

"The king's fate won't be decided here, but theirs will. Aye, and that of the island. You won't find General Mytton's terms so courteous and easy this time."

"Then let you stay at home and comfort your wife, Cheadle," called Lord Bulkeley, who had circled around, and now faced his interlocutor directly. "Or better still, stay in bed and comfort her there. She'll vouch your whereabouts, I'll warrant it."

"When the time comes, " said Sir Thomas Cheadle, "I'll stand to the line, and then we'll see if his lordship's untried sword is as valiant as his tongue."

With this, he reined his horse's head to the side and rode away. On the south side of the town, above the broad sweep of the harbour from Britons Mill towards Gallows Point, men had been digging defensive earthworks on the lower slopes of Red Hill which rose steeply above the town.

"This is where the assault will come," said Thomas Cheadle. They'll cross the strait at Porthaethwy at low tide and then camp on the summit near Cadnant."

"Would it not be better for our men to defend the higher ground first?" said Richard, his son.

"The best we can do is make a show of defending the town, and Sanders knows it, and Whitely knows it and Bulkeley, too – whatever they might say. Oh, it's a brave display on the Green, Richard, it's true, but they're no match for a trained army, and Mytton's requests for men won't be denied. Cromwell will take Wales, then he'll take Ireland, whether the King languishes at

Carisbrooke or sits on the throne in Whitehall."

As evening fell, the gathering of men dispersed. Some, near enough to home, returned to their farms and houses; some joined the garrison in the castle. Others had found billets in the town, and those who remained made shelters and lit fires near the Green, for though it was now September, the warm summer weather persisted, and it was comfortable enough to cook some meat, and quaff some ale, and lie out under the stars.

"They say they've moved the household out of Baron Hill," said Lady Anne, that evening.

"It's close to the town," replied Thomas Cheadle, noting the underlying curiosity as she talked about her old home, "and in the line from Red Hill."

"Will it be taken, do you think?"

"Who knows what may happen in the heat of battle, but I doubt it will be planned. Mytton will squeeze us with taxes but he's not a butcher."

"Do you think we will be safe here?"

He put his hand over hers. "We'll be safe."

"Even so, I've been thinking. Richard should go back to Cheshire, for a time at least. This is no place for him. Not in these times."

"Will you be the one to tell him to stop polishing his sword?"

"He's just a boy, still, Thomas. He won't know danger until it's too late. I couldn't bear it if anything happened to him."

"I'll ride at his side. I can't force him to stay here, he'd be ashamed. And it's too late now to send him home, the army is already on the march. If he met them head on, he'd want to take them on single-handed!"

It was two days later that General Mytton's army appeared. A beautiful still morning in early autumn with every detail of the mountains and the far shore as clear as crystal, and then, almost like an illusion at first, a tiny red line moving slowly along the upper shoreline at Penmaenmawr. Then, as it progressed, the image became clearer, first the cavalry, a column quarter of a mile deep, and then the infantry, all in the red coats they had worn for the first time at Naseby, a seemingly endless line, like a red snake, uncoiling itself from its lair.

"That," said Sir Thomas Cheadle to his son, "is the New Model Army."

By now the whole of the town was gathered on the Green, staring in wonder, making hardly a sound above the hushed whispers of awe and fear, whilst all the time, from the distant shore, came the steady beat of a drum, marking the time of the advancing march.

"What are you doing here, milksop!"

Richard Cheadle, who had ridden ahead of his father to get a clearer view at the front of the crowd, turned to see his namesake, Richard Bulkeley – Colonel Bulkeley, though he was no more than his own age – addressing him. "Have you come out with the bakers' boys and the milkmaids to get a good view before you run off to hide in the cellar?"

He felt his face reddening with anger, but his colour only seemed to amuse his assailant more.

"Are you tongue-tied?" he scoffed. "Ask your father, he'll tell you how he exercised his under Lady Anne's petticoats!"

"You'll feel the edge of my sword if you don't look out," muttered Richard Cheadle, aware of the weakness of his threat even as he spoke it, though he was saved further mockery by the sudden howl of someone nearby in the crowd.

At first it seemed that it might be someone taken ill with great pain, or someone suddenly teetering over the edge into insanity, but then it became clear that the person from whom the sound issued was quite deliberate in intent: some primal scream of anger and defiance being hurled across the water towards the advancing troops. A moment later, the same scream had been taken up by all those around him, and as it spread through the crowd, it assumed a terrible rhythmic insistence, accompanied, as it lasted, for some ten or fifteen minutes, by the noise of banging, sticks, pans, buckets –anything that came to hand – a terrifying din.

"They frighten themselves more than the enemy," said

Thomas Cheadle.

"Do you think they heard it, across the water?"

"It will make no difference. The scream of a Welshman is like red meat to an Englishman. But no, they'll keep their discipline."

Of the eight hundred fighting men gathered on Beaumaris Green that day, few slept well through the night which followed. Some were kept awake with excitement pulsing in their veins; some with the gut-wrench of fear; some tried to keep calm through prayer. By four o'clock in the morning all had given up any attempt to sleep further and were mustering to their positions.

Reports and rumours came back throughout the night. Some said the English army was two thousand strong, some that they had marched in single file along the mainland shore to appear more numerous than they were, knowing the enemy was watching. The earliest report from Porthaethwy was that the cavalry and half the foot soldiers had crossed the strait on the low tide the previous evening, the rest camping on the fields outside Bangor, before crossing at dawn. Further reports spoke of minor skirmishes around Porthaethwy, with madcap bands of Anglesey horsemen who were quickly scotched. By ten o'clock General Mytton's forces were gathered at the summit of Red Hill, where they drew up in order of battle.

The first advance of the English infantry towards the town was halted at two hundred yards when they came into range of the town muskets, firing with the advantage of cover from the line of earthworks at the foot of the hill. A cheer went up as three or four of the redcoats fell, and the rest retreated, albeit in orderly fashion, out of range. A further cheer went up as the Anglesey horsemen appeared, on the right flank, out of the trees, into a salient behind the infantry and the pikes.

This counterattack, led by Colonel Bulkeley, with thirty horse close behind, having the advantage of speed and surprise, seemed now about to divide a wing of the Englishmen from the main body and drive them down the hill into the range of the muskets. It was at this moment, however, that the superiority of

General Mytton's strategy emerged, for now the English cavalry, a hundred strong, charged from behind the ranks and into the Welsh horse from behind.

Chaos ensued. The muskets below, primed and ready, found themselves firing, in panic, into their own horsemen, fleeing from the charge, and six fell before the order to cease fire was heard. The rest of the horsemen, at least those not thrown, fled, and by the time the smoke had blown aside, and the cavalry had swooped away triumphantly to the left of the field, the English pike men and infantry were in a steady advance down the hill. A further volley of musket fire saw two dozen of the front-line fall, but now the advance continued, and as it drew relentlessly nearer, the time for reloading and priming grew shorter. At last, the Welsh command sounded the attack, and the rows of men, concealed in the ditches, charged.

It was a brave but desperate move. A melee of hand-fighting began and continued, seemingly without advantage, for twenty minutes; but all the time the English superiority of numbers and experience was giving them the upper hand, and suddenly, as if a dam had broken, they flooded through, and the ragged lines of Welshmen fled for safety onto the shingle of the beach, some throwing themselves into boats and pushing out into the channel, and others seeking refuge in the town. The rest, trapped in the field, four hundred in number, threw down their weapons and were taken prisoner.

Some skirmishing in the town continued. A group of desperate Welshman locked themselves in St Mary's church and fired on the English from the steeple as they made their way through the streets of the town. The remainder, with their leaders, retreated to the castle, but offered no further resistance from there.

When General Mytton came into the town, some two hours after the main fighting had ceased, he sent word to the castle to the effect that unless Colonel Bulkeley and the other officers give themselves up immediately, he would have the four hundred prisoners put to death. The ultimatum was not contested.

Richard Bulkeley and his father, Lord Bulkeley were taken to Old Place, in the town, and kept there under guard. The following day, the garrison in the castle sought honourable terms of surrender, and this was granted.

The battle of Beaumaris was over.

Thomas Cheadle and his son Richard had been with the thirty horse which attempted to surprise the enemy with their charge from the right flank of the field, just after the start of the battle. They had gathered in the woodland, near Baron Hill, and, under the cover of the trees, had observed, for two hours, the assembly of General Mytton's troops on Red Hill.

"So, whey-face," Bulkeley muttered, aside, to Richard Cheadle, "today we'll see if you're made of anything."

But in the tension of waiting, the situation was not one of personal animosities. Men waiting to fight, with life and death in the balance, share more than anything that divides them. When the moment of the charge came, they were all, in the fire of that instant, brothers.

The element of surprise was critical. As they charged from the cover, with the open field before them, and exposed to the enemy now in full view, it seemed that time stood still, and that everything, apart from the thundering of their own hooves and the beating of blood in the temples, was frozen. They were almost upon the first line of artillery, before the alarm went up, and they could see the fear in their eyes, as they broke in confusion. It was at this moment, however, just when it seemed that the manoeuvre was to be a complete success that Thomas Cheadle saw, over his right shoulder, the arc of the English cavalry, advancing towards them.

Now the confusion began to spread through their own number. Some turned, as if to face their advancing assailants, but seeing the relentlessness of the oncoming charge, reined to the side, and tried to gallop for escape. Others, riding on, seemed now to be riding into the fire from their own lines, and Cheadle saw, ten yards ahead, his own son's horse rear and fall, sending the boy sprawling to the ground.

He reined hard and jumped from the saddle, letting his horse run on. The boy was dazed but there was no sign of blood.

"Were you hit?"

"No. The horse..."

A short distance away the horse was lying with blood pouring from a wound in its throat.

"Let me see to him," said Richard, trying to stand, seemingly unaware of the imminent danger of the approaching horsemen.

"Lie still," Cheadle commanded, throwing his own weight over the boy's shoulders, protecting his head.

The ground shuddered as the hooves of the English horse thudded by; expecting to feel the slice of a sabre across the back of his neck at any moment, Cheadle lay over the boy, forcing him to be still, as still as the dead – for as such, he hoped, they would be taken.

In the first lull, and with the air full of the smoke of gunpowder, he dragged the boy to the shelter of a sill of rock protruding from the hillside turf, and then, when the centre of the battle had moved closer to the foot of the hill, he dragged him again, fifty yards to the first line of trees. There he sat, the blood pumping in his temples, his lungs burning, aware that in their scramble to safety they had passed the dead bodies of a dozen of their companions. Next to him, the boy was now retching, with long racking heaves persisting long after his stomach was empty.

"Come on," said Cheadle, when the boy had at last grown quiet, and when his own breath had eased. Though now half a mile away from the main action, it was still dangerous. If, as he suspected, the Welsh resistance did not last long, the English would be combing the ground for prisoners amongst the wounded, and for those who were still thirsty for blood, there would be some easy pickings.

After twenty minutes, they were within half a mile of Baron Hill, ground that Cheadle knew well. Between them and the house was Allt Goch Fawr, the cart track rising from the town towards Llansadryn, set in a shallow gulley between the higher tree covered ground on each side.

"Wait here," said Cheadle. "They may well have posted soldiers at the top of the lane."

He made his way cautiously through the trees, and sure enough, a hundred yards further on, a sergeant and three soldiers were keeping watch from a vantage point which gave them a clear view down the straight sloping track.

When he returned Richard was asleep. The excitement of the day and the shock of his fall had taken their toll. Nevertheless, his face had a better colour now, and so Cheadle allowed the boy's sleep to run its course. Unless the soldiers moved on, they would have to stay in concealment until darkness fell, anyway.

Half an hour later, two soldiers on horseback rode up the lane. The town had fallen, Cheadle concluded; they would be doing the rounds to update those who had been posted to the rear of the action. The horsemen did not return, but the sergeant and one of the men walked past on their way down into the town. Had Richard been fit they might make a run for it, crossing the lane and then losing themselves in the woods on the other side, around Baron Hill, but with the boy in his present state it was better to wait.

It was not far from this spot, Cheadle recalled, in the passing reverie of waiting, that he had sat in the chaise with Anne, twenty autumns ago, in the fading light, and with the air full of the smoke of bonfires, the prelude to the night they had lain together for the first time. What had ensued had created dark caves in some parts of the mind, but yet, what would he not give to have that night again!

The hours passed by. The position of the sun changed through the trees. For a time, birds were singing strongly in the afternoon light, and then it stopped. Twilight fell and the air grew chill.

"Come on, let's do it."

They slipped across the road like shadows.

There was a muttering from the two soldiers at the top of the lane, as if they had seen something in the darkness. Perhaps they thought they saw a fox or some other wild creature. Perhaps they feared a trap. Whatever, there was no pursuit.

The house was surrounded by shadowy silence, not a light from any of the windows; it was possible that someone was within, a servant or stableman left to keep an eye on things, someone who might give them succour, but they did not risk it. From the open space in front of the house, across the meadow, the church bell sounded a slow curfew.

In Llanfaes, the villagers confirmed the fall of the town. Some of the local houses had been visited by soldiers, they said, but there had been no violence. Everything had been quiet since the late afternoon.

Now following the open road, Cheadle and his son carried on towards Penmon. At the curve of the road, across the stream's ravine, the dark towers of Aberlleiniog stood out, above the trees, silhouetted in the light of a pale moon.

"They said you weren't amongst the dead," said Lady Anne. "They've been waiting for you."

"Good evening, Sir Thomas. I trust your journey home has not been too uncomfortable."

The man was not a soldier. He was clean shaven and of a pallid complexion, wearing the dark clothes of a puritan official.

"Sir Willeard Lacie," he said, announcing himself, with a very slight bow. "Parliamentary Commissioner for the Island of Anglesey."

Chapter 46

The journey from London to Beaumaris had been, for James Pennington - at least until the coach he was travelling on approached Shrewsbury - almost entirely without incident. Sitting on the outside rear basket seat as the coach made its way northwards under a grey London sky, huddled in his great-coat, he cut a sorry figure, but once the ill-effects of the rum bottle had worked their way out of his system, there was some comfort in the thought that for the best part of three days, he had only to sit here watching the countryside slip by: Barnet, St Albans, Dunstable, Towcester, Daventry, Coventry, Coleshill – some very pretty scenery, he reflected, the good English countryside, farmland and pasture, wandering rivers, gentle rounded hillsides, woodland, villages – that was the world he ought to be dealing with, not the world of cloak-and-dagger assignations, desperate rescues and such foolery.

He put it out of his mind.

The first night brought them to a coaching inn near Daventry, and after eating well, he idled away a pleasant hour sketching a handsome tavern wench with a plump and well displayed bosom, and in normal circumstances might well have tried to seize an advantage, but reminding himself, in time, that the circumstances were far from normal, he took himself to bed alone, the better to be prepared for what the following days might bring.

The beauty of the Shropshire hills brought, by the middle of the next day, a pleasing distraction, but the Welsh mountains, purple in the distance though drawing ever closer, provided a chilling reminder of the business ahead.

It was about three o'clock in the afternoon that the coachman slowed, and the passengers around him began to murmur of some kind of incident ahead. As they approached, Pennington saw that a private coach had left the track with a broken wheel. The driver had released the horse, and was tethering it to a tree, and the passenger was inspecting the damage.

As they came alongside, the driver stopped.

"Bad luck, squire. Can we take you on and leave your man here?"

"Thank you, no, dammit. But if you come across a gig five minutes ahead, tell him to keep well off this road whilst I'm about if he values his life."

"Racing you, was he?"

"A madman."

The quickest of glances confirmed to an alarmed James Pennington that the voice of the speaker, and the person of Roger Harcourt were one and the same. He turned quickly away and pulled the collar of his great-coat up around his face.

"Could have killed me, the madman."

"If I see him, I'll tell him, sir."

"When you get to the town, tell them to send a wheelwright, will you?"

"Yes. And now I'd best be onwards. The post will be no more than ten minutes behind me, now, and this is a narrow stretch of road for three or four miles yet."

Pennington heard the coachman's call to the horses, and slowly the coach moved on. Ten yards. Twenty yards. Thirty yards. And it was then, just at the point of feeling the dreadful tension lapsing from him, that he made the mistake of looking up, and caught, even at that distance, Roger Harcourt's eyes looking directly into his own.

Chapter 47

It was as the coachman said. A quarter of an hour later, the sound of galloping horses in the distance announced the approaching mail, and as it drew near, Roger Harcourt was distracted, momentarily, from the turmoil of thoughts with which he had been preoccupied since recognising, in the rear of the disappearing stage coach, the person of James Pennington.

As was the custom of the road, the driver of the mail slowed down to enquire if the unfortunate traveller by the wayside required assistance, for the road can be a dangerous place, especially for private travellers who give off any air of wealth.

"I have the means to defend myself," asserted Roger Harcourt.

The driver looked him up and down, as if respectfully questioning whether this gentleman properly understood the nature of such ruffians as, in this predicament, he might find himself having to deal with.

"Well, God be with you, sir. Make sure you're well away from here by nightfall, that's my advice."

"I intend to be," said Harcourt.

The coachman unfurled his whip, cracking it above the ears of the horses, and the coach leapt forward. As it moved away, there stood in its place, or rather, on the far side of where it had come to halt, the figure of a young man, wearing a fashionable cutaway jacket and waistcoat, with tricorn hat and pony-tail behind, a cloak over one arm, a travelling bag in the other hand.

"Daniel Flynn, sir," he said, taking off his hat and bowing his head slightly, "at your service, sir."

Chapter 48

In other circumstances, James Pennington might well have found the small Welsh seaside town of Beaumaris an agreeable place. The picturesque medieval castle, the harbour with its colourful flotilla of fishing boats, the splendid views across the Menai Strait to the Welsh mountains – all very agreeable to an artist with nothing more on his mind than his canvas and his sketchbook. In the circumstances in which James Pennington found himself, however, no place on earth could have been more oppressive.

He had taken a room at the George and Dragon on the corner of Castle Street and Church Street and had paced the length and breadth of the town for a day and a half wondering what on earth he was going to do. Having discovered the proximity of Baron Hill, he had been as far as to peer over the boundary wall, but it was a prospect that spoke to him of men and dogs, and James Pennington knew himself to be no match for men and dogs.

His best hope, he reasoned, was that Isobel would appear on the street, preferably unaccompanied, so that he could approach her; but what was his best hope was also his worst fear. She had written to him, apparently, but he had received no letter, and had certainly made no attempt to write to her, and now, here he was, with no more evidence than a scribbled note from a doctor he had never even set eyes upon that her guardian had an unscrupulous design to have her put away in a lunatic asylum.

In addition to that, Harcourt knew, or had a pretty shrewd idea, that he, Pennington, was here. What other construction could he have put on that momentary exchange of recognition on the road just outside Shrewsbury? And whatever else, Harcourt was no fool; he would have drawn up his own plan of action.

The business of the great house on the hill was, Pennington discovered in the saloon of the George, the business of the town. Sir Richard, the tenth Baronet, was expected imminently from London, and the household was to be fully re-established, which meant employment for the townsfolk and business for the tradesmen. It was rumoured, according to Joan, the landlord's wife, that Sir Richard was to re-marry, and that his fiancée, Maria's family, the Massey-Standleys, were to visit before Christmas, which would mean lavish entertainment, all good for the town. "You will have heard the sad story of his first wife, Mr Pennington – no? Lovely girl, married less than six months and she was taken, sir, God rest her soul, there's a remembrance of her in the church, if you'd care to see, a statue, well, a bust as they say, with a nice tribute, very fitting. Yes, sir, she went on, prompted by his questions, the two young ladies are still in residence, we often see them taking the air about the town, though now their guardian is arrived, I expect they're kept busy. Oh, yes, we get all the little bits of news, and his man, now there's a pretty young fellow if ever there was one, my word! But do I take it that the gentleman has an acquaintance there?"

"No," said Pennington. "No, just a passing curiosity."

"Another drink, Mr Pennington?"

"No, I'd better…"

"This one's on the house, sir."

"Oh, well, in that case. Thank you. That's very kind of you."

And so it was that, for the second day since his arrival, James Pennington spent his time listlessly roaming the streets of Beaumaris, incapable of any action apart from such as might be thrust upon him by some external agency.

Chapter 49

Ezra Lightowler, Roger Harcourt's driver and general factotum, was deeply suspicious of Daniel Flynn, the young man Harcourt had taken such a shine to on the road just outside Shrewsbury.

Daniel Flynn at your service, indeed! There was something not quite right about it if you asked Ezra Lightowler.

To begin with - for in Ezra Lightowler's opinion, the beginning was always the best place to start - the accident on the road, however he might curse about it, had been entirely Harcourt's fault. The other [no hothead] had simply made use of a natural passing place where the road widened to overtake them, and he had even raised his hat politely in doing so, but Harcourt, regarding it as a challenge, had ordered him to the chase. Now sport was one thing, and there was nothing Ezra liked more himself than a little bit of sport, but to go racing at breakneck speed along that narrow road was madness. There was nothing the other fellow could do but to accelerate further, for if they had come fully alongside and the wheels had locked, it would have been disaster for both of them. As it was, hitting a boulder at the roadside and then going onto a ditch on the other side had been a blessing. Then the first coach had stopped, and Harcourt had refused assistance, and then the second, and then the milk-faced youth standing there: *Daniel Flynn, at your service.* If suspicions had hackles, then the hackles of Ezra Lightowler's were raised from the very first moment.

It was a journey over which he had had the deepest of misgivings in the first place: going out there to the wilds of Wales to take care of the mad niece, and take her to the hospital for the mad, which, in Ezra's humble opinion, is where she should have been taken in the first place. Fighting madness with madness, Ezra said to himself, rather pleased with the analogy, and he rather wished he had someone to share it with. But he was sworn to secrecy on that point, and knowing, as he surely did, which side his bread was buttered on, it was a confidence which he had no intention of breaking.

It wasn't that he hadn't seen his master throwing caution to the wind before, mind you, wearing his head the wrong way round, as you might say; and if Ezra was less mindful of the side of his bread that had the butter on it, he might well have entertained and instructed many a gathering in the tap room of the Old Red Lion on Brick Street, where he was wont to spend an hour on his evening off, on the dangers of being too ready to part with your money at the card table, and being too fond of seeing your money riding on the back of a fickle nag, but being the soul of discretion that he was, the tap room of the Kings Head was a place where he was famous for keeping his own counsel.

But he had never known his master having a giddy spot as far as people were concerned before. Within an hour the damage to the wheel had been repaired, within two hours Harcourt had supped with his new acquaintance at a tavern in Shrewsbury, and by the time they reached Chester, lo and behold, the master had a new man! Valet, indeed! And who, one might well ask, said Ezra to himself, dreamed up that one!

If it had been a wench he'd taken a fancy to, it might have made some sense. A trim ankle, a slender waist, a pert bosom, a lively eye, now that would have been more like it, and no faithful servant begrudges his master a happy turn between the sheets, but a valet, and a callow youth to boot, that was just going too far. It was an affront, that's what it was, especially to an old retainer, for an old retainer has his sensibilities, after all.

Ezra had a shrewd eye for seeing into things, and this was a thing into which he could see more clearly than most; the fact was that the young puppy meant to fleece him, probably meant to fleece all of them, and of course, because Harcourt had a soft spot for him, for God knows what reason, he couldn't see it, and the fact was he wouldn't thank anyone for pointing it out to him. And Ezra, knowing what side his bread was buttered on, didn't intend to be the one to do it.

But he intended to keep a close eye on young Master Flynn, that's what he intended to do. At the first hint of any fleecing, he'd be down on him like a ton of bricks.

Chapter 50

James Pennington was convinced that Roger Harcourt was following him. He had seen him clearly, not thirty yards distant, on Church Street, and though he had turned away before the moment of making eye contact, he was certain that Harcourt had seen him.

His first instinct was to turn on his heels and run, but this, with an effort of will in which he took great pride, he had resisted. He turned slowly into Castle Street and stopped to glance at the window of a bookseller's for a half a minute before walking on at a leisurely pace. He then crossed the street, resisting another urge to turn and look behind him.

It was unlikely, he found sufficient presence of mind to reflect, that Harcourt would seek an open confrontation in the street, or in a shop, or any public place, and so as long as he kept on in his current mode, he had nothing to fear. On the other hand, he could not go on walking around the Beaumaris streets all day, with Harcourt a dozen paces behind him. There was the possibility of trying to double back, and slip into the George undetected, but there was a risk there, for instinct told Pennington that it would be a mistake to reveal his lodgings to Harcourt if it could possibly be avoided.

It was at this point that it occurred to Pennington to think that, quite the opposite of avoiding it, a confrontation was exactly what was required. Damn it, he said to himself, let him say to me what he has to say, and I'll say to him what I have to say, then I'll push the good doctor's letter under his nose, and demand to know what his business is here.

To this end, he walked deliberately away from the public

thoroughfare, and onto the rough meadow, in front of the castle and beside the port, which the locals referred to as 'the Green'. Here he sat down, at the head of the shingle beach, took his sketch book and a pencil out of his pocket – a nice touch, this, he thought – and began to draw.

The calmness of his outward demeanour contrasted, he fancied, rather strikingly with his inner mood, for in truth, his blood was up, and he required only the sound of Harcourt's voice, or the shadow of his figure, to provoke what, now, Pennington anticipated to be one of his finest performances.

But neither voice, nor form, nor yet shadow of form appeared, and after ten minutes Pennington turned round to discover that he was alone; the Green stretched out behind him, as far as the castle and the corner of the town, and apart from two dogs in full chase and counter chase, and a group of children trying to launch a kite, there was no-one.

The devil! said Pennington to himself, feeling relief and disappointment in equal measure, as he turned back to look at the open prospect across the strait to the shore opposite. He pictured the scene at the corner of Castle Street, with Harcourt appearing out of the crowd by the butcher's; it was definitely him, there was no doubt about it. He could picture it still: two women with baskets talking to each other, a man passing with a cart, a young fellow in a blue cutaway coat, and then, like a demon, Harcourt himself. And then for ten minutes, he had had the uncanny certainty that his antagonist was no more than a few paces behind him. At what point had he stopped following him? Or had he not followed him at all? Was his own certainty based purely on a nervous reaction to the situation?

He picked up a handful of stones and threw them one by one towards the approaching surf.

"Fine way to pass the time, if you've nothing better to do."

The voice came from some way below on the shingle where an old man was tending the moorings of a long shallow-sided boat, and Pennington recognised the amicable Welsh drollery he had found in the taproom of the George.

"I'm an artist," he said, "I'm studying the view. Very fine, too."

The old man nodded considerately, took off his cap, wiped his brow with it, and then put it back on his head.

"Now I would have put you down as a philosopher," he said, "a man of deep thoughts. That's what I would have said was your trade if you hadn't told me otherwise."

"And what about you?" said Pennington, walking towards the old man, and sitting on a wooden spar beside him. "What's your trade?"

"You see it before you," said the man, nodding towards the boat. "Ferryman, when there's anyone to ferry. When my grandfather was a boy, he could boast his grandfather was the ferryman, and when his grandfather was a boy, he could boast the same. So, there you have it, but the same won't be said by my grandson, and that's a fact."

"The bridge?"

"The bridge."

"Where do you ferry to?"

"Across to the sandbanks. You'll see them come up when the tide goes out, the Lavan sands, people have always made their own way on from there, Penmaenmawr, Conwy. The boat's made to take horses, too, you see."

"The Lavan sands."

"*Weeping* that means."

"The weeping sands?"

"That's right."

"How's that?"

"They say there was a kingdom out there, when time was, villages, farms, orchards, and then the waters came up and it was all lost to the sea. And so, the name means a lament, you see, a sorrow for something that once was that can never be again. There now, if I'm not something of a philosopher myself!"

"What do you know of the people up in the hall?"

"The Bulkeleys, you mean?"

"Yes."

"Now, then, they've been here longer than my family have

been running this ferry, I can tell you that. Some of them good, some of them bad, but what else do you expect, that's the way life is. You see, there's the philosopher in me again, it must be you that brings it out in me. But what makes you ask, are you familiar?"

"Not directly. An acquaintance of mine, acquaintances that is, are guests there, two sisters."

"Oh, yes, the two young ladies, I know who it is you speak of, I ferried them across myself, must be four weeks since. Now then, do I detect a tale of unrequited love here?"

"Ha, ha, ha!" was Pennington's repost.

"From that, I take the answer to be yes. And why not? A beggar may look at a king."

"Quite so."

"Not that I'm intimating yourself to be of the begging fraternity, you understand, except in a manner of expression, that is."

"No, the analogy is very apt. A beggar I am. But now I must let you go about your business, and I mine."

"Just one word, sir, and take it how you like. If a man wants to leave this island now, he takes the bridge, and that's what everyone expects. But if he wants to leave by, how shall I call it, clandestine or undetected means, he might still find that the old ferryman can still perform a useful service."

"Thank you," said Pennington, "I'll bear that in mind."

Somewhat cheered by his chance meeting with the ferryman, Pennington made his way back across the Green towards the town. On Castle Street, there was no sign of Harcourt and he decided it was safe now to return to the George. It was then that he became aware of a young man in a blue cutaway coat walking towards him. It was the young man he had seen on Church Street a few paces behind Harcourt. That's where he had seen the coat before. His memory was just about to locate another explanation of the coat's familiarity, when the young man spoke.

"James, where have been for the last half an hour?"

"Meg," said an astonished Pennington. "What on earth are you doing here?"

Chapter 51

On the morning of James Pennington's departure from London, after watching him - a huddled and uncomfortable figure in the outside seat of the coach - on his way, Meg Liddle returned to her room in Gooseberry Lane, and having had little rest the previous evening, fell almost immediately into a deep sleep.

Waking up at ten o'clock, she tried for a moment to extricate the strands of several different dreams which seemed to have been weaving their way through her sleeping head, all of them vaguely but now obscurely ominous, and then sat up with a sudden start, her mind achieving a stark and unwelcome lucidity.

"He won't be able to cope," she said to herself. "He'll end up getting himself into mischief."

For ten minutes, she sat in bed lamenting her own role as the prime mover in the quixotic decision to send him to Wales, a decision which was the product her own guilt as well as his. Grandmother, she said to herself, you may turn and turn as much as you may in the cramped space you've got down there, but you'll have to forgive me if I follow my inclination and not my conscience in future.

She took out the box from under the bed in which, amongst other particulars, Isobel Harcourt's letter was kept. Silly girl, she said to herself, casting it to one side as she rummaged below, this is all your fault. At the bottom of the box, she found what she was looking for, a small brass key on a string. She slipped the string over her neck, and then moved aside the bedside rug, and with a knife, prised up a loose floorboard. Reaching into the darkness beneath, she pulled out a small metal box with a lock.

The box had belonged to her grandmother, and when she died, it had contained two envelopes, each with a sum of money in it. On the first envelope was written the words 'funeral- and make it a proper one' and on the other, 'for a rainy day, and don't waste it.'

In all the years since, Meg had tried to follow her grandmother's stipulations. The funeral had been as proper as a funeral could be, with a proper coffin and a proper headstone, albeit a small one, with her name carved on it. Meg had seen to that. And though plenty of days in all those years since had seemed quite rainy enough to merit the description, she had only dipped in twice on very soggy occasions, and once in a downpour, and these only to the effect of a sovereign on each occasion. The present occasion, she decided, being a veritable deluge, she took out five guineas, which was more than half of what remained, and then locked the metal box and put it back into its place.

It was at this point, with her mind focusing and refocusing at each moment on what exactly she was proposing to do, that it occurred to her think of the blue cut-away coat, the boy's breeches, and tricorn hat which had been the costume of her latest sitting as a subject for James Pennington's canvas.

A man travelling alone from London to Wales is a traveller, no more nor less than that. A woman travelling alone from London to Wales is a matter of curiosity, and Meg knew from experience just how curious that curiosity could be. It was a risk – but then again, hadn't they said, what was it, that she was the perfect boy?

On the way to Pennington's address, she began to practise a slightly husky voice, a few casual oaths, and mildly aggressive side remarks. She stopped at a Gentleman's Outfitter at the corner of Goose Tree Lane and bought two shirts, some hose, a pair of shoes and a pair of boots - for my young brother she explained, though he's already much the same size as me. Thank you, yes, I'm sure those will fit him nicely.

From the costume trunk at the studio – which had mercifully

escaped Pennington's rampage of the previous day – she found the blue coat and the accoutrements, and hurriedly changed into them. It was fashionable for men to have sideburns and whiskers, out of the question unfortunately, but there were enough ordinary young men who still took their long hair back into a ponytail, so this she did, stretching her hair as tight as she could round the sides, and tying it behind with a simple bow. With the hat on, it looked, she judged, from her reflection in the small, cracked mirror, just about passable. She wondered about using some of Pennington's dyes or tinctures to colour her eyebrows a little darker and more manly but decided against it. She would have to do as she was.

Daniel Flynn, she said aloud, first with a sneer then with a wink, gentleman in search of his fortune, *at your service sir!*

The afternoon staging coach northward bound was full, the next after that did not leave until the following morning. The only other choice was the Post, more expensive, but non-stop.

"Eighteen hours to Holyhead, Master Flynn," the fellow boasted, and much to Meg's relief, without suspicion that his would-be traveller was anything other than the young gentleman he pretended to be.

Daniel Flynn paid for his ticket, went into the coffee house across the road, where he was able to practise a little more the mannerisms and voice of a young man, and took up his seat on the coach. His fellow travellers were, sitting opposite, a family of three, father, mother and daughter, travelling to Ireland where the father was to take up a post in the customs, and to her left, a large man of fifty who slept and snored for the whole journey, waking up with a start every twenty minutes or so, saying 'Bless my soul', before dropping off again.

"Are you travelling far, young sir?" enquired the father of the family.

"Daniel Flynn, sir," he said, extending his hand in a purposeful manner. The man shook his hand and introduced his family.

"As far as Menai Bridge," said Daniel, returning to the original question. "Then to Beaumaris. My Master had to set out before me, leaving me to complete some business for him. Now I am to join him there."

"Very good, very good," said the man, who had a robust and good-humoured manner. "A good valet is the crown jewel of a gentleman's household. And how old might you be, Master Flynn?"

"Seventeen," said Daniel, choosing an age which, she hoped, would suggest youthfulness as the reason for less obvious masculine attributes.

"Seventeen," said the man, approvingly. "Well, you've got your whole life ahead of you. I would that I were seventeen again!"

"Father!" said the daughter, with affectionate reproval.

"Bless my soul!" said the sleeping man in one of his moments of remission. The girl, sitting opposite, giggled, and caught Daniel's eye, with a mirthful twinkle.

Dusk began to settle. The coach stopped at St Alban's to change horses, and the passengers had twenty minutes to take their refreshment. Then they were on their way again, and there was some further desultory conversation until, with darkness now closing around, silence descended on the company as the coach hurried on through the night.

The large man to Daniel's left seemed now to have found an altogether deeper and sounder level of continuous sleep, and his snores and snorts and occasional 'bless my souls' were now replaced by a steady and contented drone; to this was added the deep and leathery breathing of the *pater familias* and the lighter, more tuneful and genteel suspirations of his spouse, all of them mingling into a rhythmic foreground of sound against the clatter of sixteen hooves and the monotonous rumbling of four sturdy wheels.

A single candle, flickering in its glass lantern which swayed with the motion of the coach, threw a low ghostly light over the sleeping forms and faces, and Daniel became aware, not immediately but over a period of time, as various seemingly random incidences began to form a pattern, that the girl opposite, the daughter of the family, was attempting to catch his eye with winning looks.

He turned his head aside, as if to look out of the window into the dense blackness but that had the additionally disconcerting effect of providing a mirror, however imperfect, into the compartment, and that mirror, reflecting the opposite window, provided a second even less perfect mirror in which he could see himself and the girl as if they were people who belonged to a separate and unrelated world.

And just as a cough becomes all the more ticklish and insistent when there is some overriding reason not to cough, so Daniel Flynn found now a most provocative compulsion to submit his eye to a tentative exchange of glances. He looked upwards above her head, then looked downward towards his own knees, and then reversed the process, this time finding the two eyes opposite firmly engaging with his own for a brief moment before setting off, so very becomingly, on their own orbit again. A moment later, the same again, only this time the look dwelt a little more lingeringly, a little more tellingly, before assuming another guise of perfect innocence.

Now a young man of Daniel Flynn's tender years and limited experience of the world might well have been perplexed at such an unusual look and might well have wondered what it meant; a young woman of Meg Liddle's experience of the world, however, knew exactly what it meant, for it was a look that she had used herself in situations enough where an unspoken message had to be delivered.

It was a look which conveyed vulnerability, and at the same time paid a subtle compliment to its recipient; it was a look which combined the most delicate hint of femininity with a distinct and provocative boldness. It was a look, in short, which was designed to set the blood racing.

In the present circumstances, though it might confirm certain aspects of the illusion of Daniel Flynn that Meg Liddle might well be reassured to have confirmed, it was also the cause of considerable alarm, and not something which could wisely be allowed to continue any longer. Meg Liddle closed her eyes as if to go to sleep, and a short time later, Daniel Flynn let out as dry and unattractive a snore as he could muster to join the serenade that already filled the compartment. And soon after that, the masquerade of sleep became the thing itself.

When he next opened his eyes, the pale light of a sickly dawn was seeping along the eastern horizon, and those within the coach were variously preoccupied with the discomforts and aches and pains which had accumulated during a night of thin and unreplenishing sleep. Another change of horses at Daventry, another brief respite from the rigours of the journey, and the travellers took their positions again. The large man sitting next to Daniel, having now, it would seem, been drained of every last drop of sleep, began to make conversation, and the chief topic of his conversation, it soon became clear, was his own state of health, which was, as he assured the company, decidedly and chronically poor, though nevertheless a matter of the greatest interest, not least to his own physician, who, he informed them, regarded him as an encyclopaedia of ailments and symptoms from which the world at large might derive great edification and profit.

The pater and mater familias, having symptoms and ailments of their own which they were quite happy to share, the conversation thrived for some time on matters of gout, liverish debility, scrofulous necks and lumbago and rheumatics, and malevolent humours, until by force majeure it declined at last into a monologue, and the main speaker finally rediscovering, through his effort, the call of Morpheus returning, he closed his eyes, drooped his head, and a new silence fell on the compartment.

During all this time, Daniel Flynn was aware that the damsel opposite, far from entertaining amorous thoughts, was now sitting with a fixed and severe look, and whenever the line of their eyes crossed, it was to convey, from her to him, a look of deepest disapproval. Daniel Flynn, inexpert in the ways of love, might well have wondered what promise had been broken, or advantage taken; Meg Liddle, however, had no such consternation. A woman has only so many weapons in her armoury, and it was quite in order to practise with them at any opportunity to keep them sharp and fit for use.

The morning was now fully advanced. The coach sped on through the countryside of Shropshire. Another five hours would bring them to Bangor. Ahead, a coach had broken down by the side of the road. The coach slowed down, and the inhabitants heard the brief conversation between the driver and the fellow by the roadside. Recognising the voice, and then standing to view the profile of Roger Harcourt, Meg Liddle saw a new and unlooked for opportunity.

"It's my master," Daniel Flynn announced to the company, and with that he plucked his bag from beneath the seat, opened the door and stepped down.

Chapter 52

Mr Harcourt was walking privately in the grounds with his valet, Daniel Flynn, and it was something that Ezra Lightowler - watching from the little parlour which was part of the servants' quarters - did not like one little bit. Ezra Lightowler had heard that there were people who were so adept in the art of deciphering the movements of a person's lips that the meaning thereof could be construed without a sound being heard, and he truly wished that he had devoted a little of his own time to the cultivation of that skill, for there was, as far as he could see, a considerable amount of lip moving going on between Mr Harcourt and Master Flynn and he would dearly like to know what the matter of it was.

"He's a pretty young fellow, and no mistaking!" said Jane, the kitchen maid. "He's got all the young servant girls talking!"

"Has he indeed?" said Ezra, rather resenting the interruption to his concentrated observation of the scene from the little window.

"Oh yes, that he has. Not me, mind you."

"Really, is that so?" said Ezra, watching as his master and Flynn descended the step from the terrace, and walked away through the formal gardens.

"Oh, yes. I like a fellow with a bit more brawn about him, a bit more manliness is more to my taste, if you know what I mean."

Turning from the window, Ezra took the sudden suspicion that such brawn as she might be referring to was exactly the same kind of brawn of which he, Ezra Lightowler was possessed. Now, what Mrs Lightowler, the lady, that is, who had owned that name by virtue of marriage to him these twelve years, might think of this, he did not know, or rather he did know, but then Mrs Lightowler was a very long way away in London, and he was a very long way away in Wales, and nature is nature when all's said and done.

"Would I be correct in assuming," he said, turning from the window and noticing the somewhat floury appearance of the kitchen maid's apron and the tip of her nose, "that there's pastry in the making."

"Pastry there is," was her reply.

"Would I also be correct in assuming, then," he continued, "that we are to have pies?"

"Correct again," said the maid, who seemed in no way displeased to be thus interrogated, and it struck Ezra Lightowler that this felicitous line of questioning might well be harnessed to lead into all manner of topics, when, in the corner of his eye, he saw Roger Harcourt and Daniel Flynn reappearing from the ornamental stairway to the upper terrace. The master was still talking to the man, and Ezra observed as he tapped him on the shoulder. Then, the so-called valet turned on his heel and set off in a sprightly manner, as one who has just been despatched on an errand.

"You must excuse me," said Ezra, hurrying to the kitchen door and pulling on his hat; and thus it was that, without discovering the nature of the filling of the pies, whether sweet or savoury, nor yet finding out whether or not they were already in the oven, Ezra Lightowler set out in pursuit of Daniel Flynn.

The fellow was a good hundred yards ahead by the time Ezra caught sight of him between the trees of the avenue, and it was all the coachman could do to maintain that distance, for the scoundrel was fleet of foot it had to be admitted.

At the lodge, he turned away sharply, evidently taking the steps down to Allt Goch Fawr, the road coming up the hill from the town towards Llansadryn, passing under the arched bridge he had just crossed, and which Ezra Lightowler now approached. Looking down from the parapet he saw the fellow once again, now hot-footing down the hill in the direction of the town.

It was a steep road, and very straight for the first quarter of a mile, and so Ezra had to keep to the side of the road where the shadow of the boundary wall afforded him some concealment. Then, just where the lines of cottages began to appear on each side, the road curved first one way and then the next, and with people and carts and barrows now between him and his prey, he was able to break into a slight trot to keep him in sight and make up a little ground.

Then, a hundred yards before reaching the centre of the town, where Church Street and Castle Street meet, the fellow turned sharply to the right and went up the steps that led through a gate into the churchyard.

Ezra Lightowler stopped for a moment, long enough to take a grubby kerchief from his pocket and wipe his brow and began the following dialogue with himself:

"Now, Ezra, why would the rogue go into a church?"

"Not to communicate with his maker, Ezra, not if I have any insight into human nature."

"Then for what other reason might the scoundrel go in there?"

"You might not be far wrong, Ezra, if you surmised that the reason had something to do with an assignation?"

Pleased with this piece of deduction, for Ezra's motive for following him had nothing more particular than to discover something suspicious, he stepped into the churchyard and proceeded as far as the porch. Despite applying the lightest touch of which he was capable, the church door latch opened with a heavy metallic echo, but it took only a few moments for him to ascertain that there was no-one within.

Closing the door behind him, he stepped out of the porch, looked both ways, and then continued to follow the path around the church. He expected to find an enclosed churchyard on the far side but instead discovered that another entrance gate led away to a street beyond, and it was through that gate that he now hurried, certain that Daniel Flynn had passed there no more than a few moments before.

Almost immediately, he stopped dead in his tracks, finding

himself in the shadow of a daunting stone-built giant of a structure which he immediately recognised as a gaol. In London, where Ezra Lightowler knew the layout of the roads as well as he knew the lines on his own hand, it was always possible to avoid choosing a route which passed directly by a gaol, and it was his habit to do so, having such a morbid dislike of prisons that he regarded even getting close to one as a dangerous taunt to providence, and it was for this reason that he had to stand still, for a moment, in order to sustain the deep shudder of misgiving which penetrated to the very marrow of his bones. And if the massiveness of the stone walls was not enough, his eye now caught a doorway high up on the end wall underneath which he was standing. It was a doorway which had no steps leading up to it, a doorway, which, Ezra judged, was intended not for a man to enter, but for a man to exit never to return, in other words, a hangman's doorway; before the deep shudder had fully passed, an icy chill now sent tentacles of fear through his veins, and it was only through a huge effort of will that he managed at last to resume his mission.

Turning into the cold shadowy street which ran alongside the gaol wall, he caught sight of Daniel Flynn, now fifty yards ahead. Breaking now into a shuffle, for he realised that unless he made some headway to catch him up he could easily lose him in the twists and turns of the surrounding streets, he reached the end of the prison wall, turned, turned again, and once more saw Flynn, now making his way along the road on the other side of the gaol.

Doubling back, said Ezra to himself, *must have an inkling someone's after him. Either that, or he's lost.*

Ten minutes later, he found himself, having it seemed sweated off a good portion of that brawn with which the kitchen maid had been so impressed, back in churchyard, and there was no sign of his quarry.

Dammit if he hasn't given me the slip! said Ezra Lightowler.

He took off his hat, scratched his head, looked disconsolately around, this way and that, and then made his way off.

As soon as he had gone, Daniel Flynn slipped out from behind the gravestone where he was hiding and made his way to the taproom of the George and Dragon.

James Pennington was already there, sitting by the fire.

"Get me a mug of ale and a pipe," said Meg, clearing her throat noisily for the benefit of the company and spitting into the fire

"Well?" said Pennington.

"He wants me to arrange a meeting."

"Between himself and me?"

"No. Between you and her."

"What? With Isobel?"

"Yes."

"To what purpose?"

"He wants you to run away with her. That's what he wants."

Chapter 53

Contrite, meek, calm, apologetic, remorseful, wistful – Meg Liddle struggled to find exactly the right combination of words to describe the manner in which Roger Harcourt had expressed the quandary in which he found himself with regard to his ward. A man alone with a stranger will sometimes open up his mind and his conscience in ways that would be impossible with those with whom he is familiar by circumstance and routine.

"I have been harsh, too harsh, I fear. Out of concern for her well-being, I have set obstacles in her way and compromised the natural and tender feelings that should exist between us. I have been too protective, too severe. I have denied the power of love. I see it now, in these beautiful and serene surroundings, in ways which I could not before."

"Why not let them meet in the normal way of society?" his valet suggested.

"I fear that my motives would be doubted in any such proposal. Is it not a sad thing when a man cannot do good in spite of his own best intentions."

"You are determined, then, to let her have her liberty?"

"I am determined to let her test the strength of her feelings. Then, in good time, I will seek reconciliation."

"And how is this to be done?"

"It is in this that I must trust in your discretion and put you to service. You must speak to Isobel and make it known to her that he has come to seek her out but impress upon her the need for utmost secrecy. Then, find the man - you've seen him once, you'll have no difficulty recognising him. Gain his confidence with the earnestness of your intentions, then be the facilitator of their plan. Do it how you like. I'll not interfere. Leave her sister to me. I'll console her and reconcile her in good time."

"Let me go into the town now, then," said the valet, "and find out where he lodges. If I am to gain his trust, I need to make myself known to him as soon as it may be done."

"Very well," said Harcourt.

"And then," Meg continued, spitting again into the fire of the parlour of the George and Dragon, "his buffoon of a driver took it into his head to follow me, so I had to shake him off before I could get here."

"So, just let me make sure I understand this. He now wants her to run away with me?"

"That's the plan I've been charged with."

"What if she refuses? It's been six months; she may well have changed her mind."

"There were letters, apparently, from her to you, intercepted somehow. Violent protestations of love. The letters were probably shown to the doctor who wrote to you."

"Really! Violent protestations of love! And so you think he's come round."

"He says he has."

"And you doubt it?"

"Don't you?"

"What motive could he have?"

"Shall I tell you what I think?"

"Go on."

"I think he wants further proof of her madness. Lord Bulkeley arrives within the next few days. What better way of vindicating his wish to have his ward put away than to have someone as eminent as Lord Bulkeley confirm his story."

"My God! What on earth am I to do now?"

"We need to think it through carefully."

"Or just cut and run."

"No. You can't do that. We know that he means to have her put away anyway, and I'm sure that's what he'll do. He thinks the situation has played into his hands. That's the advantage we have over him. The only way to discredit him is to demonstrate that this scheme is a deliberate ploy on his part."

"But how can we do that?"

"Let me think on it. In the meantime, you need to plan how you can get away from the island."

"With her, you mean?"

"With her or without her. I don't know yet."

"The ferry," said Pennington. "I made the acquaintance of the ferryman the other day."

"That might serve. I'll go back to the house now, tell him we've met and that I've persuaded you that it's all honourable and above board."

"You're a true friend, Meg!"

Meg coughed noisily, hoping thereby to divert any attention from the reference to her female name.

"What?" said Pennington. "Oh, right, I see!"

Chapter 54

1649

At the time of the execution of King Charles, a sense of shock and outrage ran through the country, felt as much by those who had opposed him, as those who championed his cause. The pitiful groan of ordinary folk who witnessed the event in Whitehall was echoed, as the news spread, up and down the land. Whatever it was all about, whatever privations had to be suffered, however ill-advised the king, however indiscreet or sinful, however arrogant, it was not meant to lead to this.

On Anglesey, with its centuries of loyalty to the crown, the sorrow was heart-felt, and it bristled, here and there, into anger and talk of revolt. But it was only talk.

In the immediate wake of the surrender of Beaumaris, under the terms of General Mytton's order for the reduction of the island, the rumour was of sequestration of the island's estates. In the negotiations which now took place between the new Governor of Beaumaris Castle, the parliamentary commissioners, and the representatives of the landowners, the alternative which was offered was the levy of a shilling for every pound of an estate's worth, or the equivalent of two years' income, and articles were drawn up accordingly.

Such stinging penalties were not lightly forgotten, and though those who had cooperated most with the administrative regime which followed Mytton's victory were vilified by their fellows, there were few who truly believed that an alternative existed.

It did not surprise Thomas Cheadle that he was accounted one of the foremost collaborators, and as a man who had long ceased courting popularity, it did little to ruffle his self-esteem. Facts were facts, and if those who liked the sound of their own voices ranted until they were blue in the face, it did not alter the fact that Anglesey now had to get itself steady on its own feet again and live with the times. If he gained favour with his new political masters, and if he consolidated his own family's wealth and security, that was his business. The wilder rumours, such as the allegation that his son, Richard, had somehow slipped away to Porthaethwy to organise crossings for Mytton's soldiers on the eve of the battle, he dismissed with contempt.

For some time after the king's death, there was a nervousness amongst the authorities in London - always wary of the Welsh - that there might be further insurrection in Anglesey and North Wales. In June of 1649, it was reported that a Captain Rich, of the *Rebecca*, had anchored during the night off Fryars', landing men and arms which had been accommodated at Lady Cheadle's Fort, as Aberlleiniog Castle had come, somewhat contemptuously, to be known.

In reality, the number of men landed, and billeted overnight, was no more than ten. They were due to join the small garrison at the castle, not with any offensive strategy in mind – the arms they carried were not weapons but tools – but to assist in the process of rendering the castle unfit, effectively, for any further military purpose.

It had been decided – and agreed by Cheadle – that the landing of the men at Fryars' Road would cause less alarm than if they landed at the harbour in Beaumaris itself, but notwithstanding, the affair gained notoriety in the region, and served further to alienate Cheadle from his fellow islanders.

In the autumn, Cheadle was visited by his stepdaughters and their husbands.

It was not a social visit.

"Tell them I'm ill," said Anne, wearily, retiring to her chamber.

It was Mary, always the most vociferous, who began, "After everything else, you now set your own advancement above that of your fellow countrymen and the king."

"At the present moment," Cheadle reminded them, "there is no king."

"That's the kind of comment I might have expected!"

"It's a very significant fact."

"The shame you bring on the family is something we have to put up with, do you realise that?"

"I must do what I think is right."

"Where is my mother?"

"Not well."

"In what way not well? May I see her?"

"She doesn't wish to see you."

"This is all your doing," said Mary, bitterly. "From the start."

It was not just Cheadle himself who suffered this kind of treatment. Richard was not spared by his old tormentor, Richard Bulkeley.

"They say you're turning puritan, Cheadle. What will you be, a Quaker? Good choice, I'd say. Or maybe a Leveller. You know how to measure your level along the turf, don't you? Take your hat off, Cheadle, let's see if you've shaved your head yet."

"For myself," said Anne, "I care not, but for Richard, this isn't fair. He can't show his face in the town without ridicule, and it's all undeserved."

"He says he doesn't care."

"He says so. But it does. It affects him, I can tell."

"What should I do, send him away?"

"Maybe it would be for the best."

"I'll speak to him. Perhaps he should do what I once thought of doing."

Anne smiled wanly, knowing what he meant, and remembering, too, that it was her influence that had prevented him.

Chapter 55

The time hangs heavy for a man waiting to achieve a great purpose, and James Pennington was such a man.

Whatever the treacherous machinations of Roger Harcourt, whatever the complications of Meg's counterplan, James Pennington had it in his head that it was only a matter of hours before he was to be re-united with Isobel Harcourt, and he anticipated that event with the eagerness of a bridegroom.

This time there would be no hesitation, no moment of indecision and uncertainty, no moment of doubt. Never had Pennington had a stronger sense of conviction. He tried to summon to his memory Isobel Harcourt's image, but strangely, though he could recall each detail of his painting of her, the true living details of her face eluded him.

That, however, would soon be over.

He had his plan. Once away from the island, he would take her to Chester, then to Liverpool, then to New York. They would start a new life in America. He would apply his skills to some honest trade, a carpenter or a decorator or a designer of buildings, and would try his fortune there, where opportunity was free to all men.

There was business, however, to be dealt with first, and with that in mind, he went to visit his friend the ferryman.

"It seems that I may need your services, after all," he said.

The ferryman looked warily around. "Now, you see, the thing is…" he began, in a cautious voice, "I've had the constable of the watch here this very morning, and he said to me that though I may take a man across if he requests it, or a woman across if she requests it, I must not take a man and a woman across together, especially if the man is of a description that resembles yourself, you see, but I must say that the tide is not quite right, or the wind is not quite right, and hold them here, then raise the alarm."

This, Pennington reflected, bore the hallmark of Harcourt's plan as Meg had described it: let her get as far as here - by which time she's condemned herself - and no further.

"Can they stop you doing your business?"

The old man shrugged.

"Your licence, then, I suppose?"

"Not that there's any trade to speak of. But the cottage, now..."

"That goes with the licence, I take it?"

He nodded.

"Did you say anything? About me I mean."

The old man shook his head then made a gesture to show that silence was his stock in trade.

"I'll have to find another way. Any suggestions?"

"You could go to Amlwch, get a boat to Ireland. Or make a dash for Porthaethwy, cross over the bridge. Anyone in pursuit, though, well, without a start, you've no chance."

"The case is hopeless, then."

"Have you ever walked any further along this shore?"

"No further than here."

"Well, then. Let me tell you something that might interest you. If you walk on another half mile, the shore curves away, goes under some cliffs. Now, just before you get there, you'll come across a tender, a small rowing boat, that is. Mine, though I've not been out in it for five years. You'd not want to trust it on the open sea, but it's fit for one more passage across the water. Take it, if you've a mind to. When you're done, just cast her off. If they find an empty boat," he laughed, "that'll give them something to think about!"

"My friend," said Pennington, "let me give you some money for your kindness."

The old man raised his hand. "If you give me money and you take my boat, sir, it might be taken that you give me money *for* my boat, sir, and that makes me your accomplice. If you don't give me money, and you take my boat, that makes you a thief. Then it will be on your conscience and not mine, you see, and that's the way I'd like to keep it."

"Thank you," said Pennington. "Now I can say that for once in my life I met a good man, and because of that, I'll try to do some good in the world myself. So, goodbye."

Chapter 56

26th October 1831

It has been with considerable difficulty that the events of the last twenty-four hours have been concealed from Isobel. Mr Harcourt, our guardian, has departed once more for London, and though we have been assured by Lord Bulkeley of the purity of his motives, considerable doubt remains in my own mind as to his veracity in some respects.

My understanding of what happened during the night is far from complete, most of it gathered from fragments overheard of conversations in which I was an eavesdropper rather than a participant.

I was summoned to the drawing room alone before breakfast. As I approached, I became aware that Lord Bulkeley and Mr Harcourt were in private conversation, and as I waited at the open doorway, I overheard his lordship saying the following: "As far as the doctor's letter is concerned, his death renders it invalid, and the manner of his death must call into question the state of his mind and indeed his judgement."

I was considering the significance of this when his lordship saw me and beckoned me in. I was instructed to make arrangements for Isobel to be taken out for the day.

"Who normally accompanies you on your outings?"

"Thomas."

"Then let him go with you."

"Is Daniel to be permitted to accompany us?"

I detected from his lordship's long drawn breath, and my guardian's turning away that, in whatever had happened, Daniel had had some part to play, and not a part for which he might expect to have any praise.

As I left the room, I lingered a little, just long enough to hear Lord Bulkeley saying, "Now listen to me, Harcourt, this business has got to stop, do you hear me?" and there was a note in his voice quite sufficient to convey marked displeasure.

I told Isobel, who was still at her dressing table, that an excursion was proposed for us, and returned to the drawing room, partly to tell them that my task was done, and partly, I admit, to see if I could glean any further information. It was for this reason that I was tempted, once more, as I approached the doorway, to linger for a moment unseen. The brief fragment I heard caused a chill to run down my spine. "If any injury comes to light, or even worse, a fatality, there'll be serious charges to answer. I'll have men sent to the mainland coast to see if any landing's been reported. Meantime, I think you would do well to prepare for a speedy return to London. Should you need to return here for an inquiry or any such thing, I will send word."

I heard my guardian's footsteps and made that my moment to enter. He walked past without looking at me.

His lordship turned from the window, as I approached, and I took the opportunity to ask, "Am I allowed to be told what has happened?"

His lordship paused to consider, then gestured for me to sit down.

"It was feared that your sister had made an attempt to elope during the night."

"But she was asleep in bed."

"Yes. Unfortunately, before the simple expedient of checking on that simple fact was tried, supposition, and, I fear, some degree of expectation had already led events on."

"Expectation?"

"You know your sister's history as well as anyone. I presume you also know that the man who was the object of her misplaced affection had travelled here to Beaumaris for purposes which we must assume were to do with renewing his suit to her."

"Yes, my guardian said as much to me, though he also made

it a matter of the highest importance that Isobel was to have no knowledge of it."

"Yes, indeed. However, by Mr Harcourt's account, his suspicion was that she knew of it notwithstanding."

"And am I to understand that some action was taken?"

"Suffice it for the moment to know that she is safe and that the danger itself is now removed. You may judge that I am not altogether convinced that your guardian has dealt with the matter wisely; there is one respect, however, in which I am inclined to agree with him. Isobel must be protected from any knowledge that would cause her anxiety. She appears to me, at least in the short time that I have been here, in a perfectly healthy state of mind, but there is no doubt, as you have agreed yourself, that she has undergone a great deal of suffering, and at all costs, she must be spared anything that might jeopardise her current equanimity."

With this, he gave me to understand that our conversation should be regarded as complete, and he told me that he would go directly to see Thomas to make arrangements for our excursion.

We were taken to Penmon, a little further along the coast from Lleiniog, a place noted, by those touring Anglesey, for its ruined priory. Close to the priory, there is a dovecote, equally ancient, a pond which, as Thomas informed us, was stocked with fish for the acolytes who dwelt here, and a spring-fed well where, legend has it, the saint himself once had his cell. Immediately behind the priory, on the hillside above, there is a church and living, with a churchyard containing graves from our own and the last century.

At a distance of about a mile – which distance we walked, in a blustery wind - is Penmon Point, where the coastline changes direction, and opposite the small but very distinctly shaped island which is known variously as Priestholme or St Seirol's island, names which gives an indication of its former purpose, though now, we are told, it is inhabited only, apart from the many species of seabird, by a keeper and his family.

The coast is very rugged here, and the sea currents between

the point and the island are turbulent, exposed as they are to winds from contrary directions. Ships attempting to pass through this narrow channel do so at great risk, Thomas informed us, and many, over the years, have run into trouble, not always without loss of life.

Isobel and Thomas were united in praising the romantic atmosphere that attaches both to the priory and to the adjacent coast, and I, too, was sensible of this quality, but because I was preoccupied with other matters, I was not able to open myself to its influence quite so fully as I might otherwise have done. Uncertainty about last night's events was one aspect of my perplexity; the other, and in the privacy of a diary, if only there, I may admit it, was Daniel. Had he made up one of our party, I know my spirits would have been lighter, but the prospect now – if he has not departed already – is that he will depart with Mr Harcourt, and that possibly we will see him no more. My thoughts are fanciful, I know, but I shall miss him more than I care to admit. I fear I am destined always to be luckless in affairs of the heart!

As I suspected, by the time we returned, Mr Harcourt had already taken his leave and had begun his journey back to London. Isobel said that she would retire to her room to read before dinner, and so I found myself alone.

I have often observed that in matters of household business, there is no-one so likely to have a complete and comprehensive acquaintance with the facts as the domestic staff, and with this in mind, I ventured to the kitchens, and searched out Jane, who I know to be a willing and unguarded chatterer, and it did not take a great deal of prompting to persuade her to give me the benefit of the knowledge she has of last night's events.

Her account was somewhat tortuous, but I have done my best to render an account of it, though I struggled somewhat to find an adequate form of punctuation to render its meaning clear!

"Well, miss, it's a to-do, it is, and no mistake about it, I don't know what to make of it, or who to believe or who not to believe, well, from what I've heard there was two or three of them with guns, but Mary, now, she says it was just one, but the watch was armed too, though some of them just with pieces fit for clearing chimneys, on account of information they had that he was armed, and they lay in wait for him, or them, for some people say there was a woman, too, but he didn't come where they expected, and so, well it was later on that the shots were fired near where the old ferry was, and old Len says that if there was an abduction about it, or a habeas corpus or some such thing about it, then shots can be fired within the law, and Mary says she heard they were killed outright, but Ezra - Mr Lightowler - says it was too dark to see."

"Mr Lightowler?" I interrupted. "What was he doing there?"

"Well, he was with Mr Harcourt, of course, but he wouldn't say any more, you see he knows his lordship is not pleased that there was any shooting at all, but more than that he will not say. Well maybe Mr Harcourt knew the man, or maybe money was owed, who's to tell, though usually there's money somewhere near when people fall to blows, or love, and some people say a woman was seen coming down the hill and turning into the graveyard but it's my belief that that was just a ghost returning home, but where young Mr Daniel is, no-one knows, or no-one tells, which is two different things, but Mr Lightowler thinks there was always something not quite right there, and he's not the only one to think so, but nothing's been seen of him and some thinks he'll be seen no more, which is good riddance if you ask me, not that you do, but there it is, anyway, and if you ask me something else, if your Mr Harcourt meant to have your sister put away for a mad woman, there's something not quite right there either, but who am I to have an opinion on such a matter?"

"Who told you this?" I cried in astonishment.

Here she paused, almost for the first time in her meandering discourse. "Ezra…Mr Lightowler. miss," she said, at last, her face turning scarlet. "Sorry, miss, have I said something I shouldn't, miss?"

"No, Mary," I said, recovering my equanimity, at least on the surface, for her benefit, though my mind was racing to piece together the fragments of conversation between Mr Harcourt and his Lordship which I had overheard and which hitherto had remained obscure.

Had he not already departed, I would certainly have confronted my guardian directly with this dreadful accusation; in his absence, however, and because I knew that I could not rest until I had confirmation or otherwise, I decided to be so bold as to seek some clarification from Lord Bulkeley.

I judged from his immediate reaction that the matter was one which had already been a cause of some disquiet to him, and that perhaps he had hoped to avoid discussing it directly with me.

"Whatever you have heard," he said, after pausing for some moments to consider his reply, "I think we must accept that your guardian acted, howsoever ill-advisedly, from the best of motives. However, he has taken my advice to return to London, and I am confident that there will be no further interference with your sister's affairs. In addition, and I would have spoken to you on this matter as soon as a suitable opportunity presented itself, I intend to offer your sister my protection here for the foreseeable future, at least that is until she reaches her majority, and then she may make decisions for herself. I hope it will meet with your approval to stay here also as her companion."

"That is most kind of you," I said, not quite able to conceal my pleasure and embarrassment.

"My motives are not entirely selfless. Maria will be spending time here at Christmas, and during the spring, in preparation for our wedding next August; it will be a relief to me to know that there will be such agreeable companionship for her."

"In that case, I am sure that Isobel, and certainly myself…"

"I think perhaps that we should first allow a few days to pass before putting this to your sister. That way, it will seem more of a natural thing, rather than one arising out of a crisis. Do you agree?"

I assured him that I did.

"Is something going on?" said Isobel, after dinner. "And why has Mr Harcourt travelled back to London so unexpectedly?"

"You remember Dr Fairhurst?"

"How can I ever forget him!"

"Mr Harcourt had word that he died in rather unhappy circumstances. His Lordship knew of this but at first did not realise we were acquainted with him."

"Rather unhappy circumstances?"

"His body was taken out of the river."

"Oh no! Poor man."

"Yes, I know. It's a terrible thing."

"He was a strange man, but I'm sure his heart was kind underneath. And is that why everyone is in such a state?"

"Oh, there was some fuss in the town last night. I'm not quite sure what. Some fellow trying to escape from the gaol."

"Good heavens! Did they catch him?"

"Yes. But people are a bit unsettled. His lordship thinks it best if we stay out of the village for a few days, at least."

"Perhaps we can go on another excursion. Thomas says there is a very fine beach at Red Wharf, which is not far from here, apparently."

I agreed, relieved to find her in so serene a mood, judging that the attempt to protect her from any distressing knowledge regarding Mr Pennington has been successful.

27th October 1831

I completed my account of yesterday's events late last night, and now, a day later, I have only one further episode to add before I seal this diary forever and hide it away where no-one but myself – perhaps not even I – will ever have cause to see it again.

I did not include in yesterday's entry the minor inconvenience we suffered when, preparing for our outing to Penmon, Isobel was unable to find her cloak and shoes. It was simple enough for me to let her have the use of my own spare cloak, which happened to be at hand, and she easily found some other shoes suitable for walking. Later, she remembered that she had sent the items down to be cleaned after our previous outing.

After breakfast this morning, I went down to the laundry room to retrieve the items for her, thinking that perhaps they had been put to one side and overlooked amidst all the busy preparations for his lordship's return. The laundrymaid, however, remembered the items clearly.

"Bless, my soul, yes. James cleaned the shoes and I did the cloak myself. They were ready days ago."

"Are they still here?"

"No. I gave them to Mr Harcourt's man, Daniel, along with some other things belonging to Miss Harcourt. He said he would make sure they were returned to her."

"Daniel took them?"

"Yes. Did I do wrong, miss?"

"No."

I turned away, conscious of the flush on my own cheek, and hurried to Isobel's room to ascertain what other items of clothing were missing. Even before I reached the stairs, however, the truth began to dawn on me. I pictured Daniel dressing in Isobel's cloak and gown and leaving the house, during the night, and understood, albeit obscurely, something of his role in the events of two days ago. That, however, was not the prime cause of my consternation, it was the sudden shock of realising that the young man who was my guardian's valet, the young man for whom I had felt the tender affections of my heart stirring, was no man at all, nor ever had been.

Chapter 57

The reputation of being a man with whom a secret could be entrusted was one Ezra Lightowler was justly proud of. In normal circumstances, he knew himself to be as tight-lipped as a clam, and people might wink, or nudge his elbow, or offer him a drink, or any other type of inducement, and tight-lipped as a clam he would remain. He liked to think that under duress, as in a rigorous interrogation, even with the threat of more extreme measures, he would remain true to his character. But every man has his price, or his weakness, and a man who wishes to impress a woman may, in the heat of the moment, succumb to such a weakness, and undergo a short-lived confusion as to the side on which his bread is buttered.

The blush which had accompanied Mary, the kitchen-maid's disclosure to Emily, that her sister was to be taken away for a madwoman, might well have derived from her sense of revealing something she had promised to keep secret; it may well also have been a blush deriving from her recollection of the business which had followed shortly after becoming possessed of this knowledge, a business which, had she known of it, Mrs Lightowler, many miles away in London, would certainly have disapproved.

Travelling back to London with Mr Harcourt, and, on the whole, very glad to be doing so, especially in the knowledge that Daniel Flynn had uttered his last *at your service* to his master, Ezra Lightowler was just as conscience stricken at his own lapse from the high principles of confidentiality as from the high principles of marital fidelity, but he resolved, nevertheless, that just as he had succeeded, for many years, in keeping Mr

Harcourt's dark secrets from the scrutiny of the world, he could certainly keep his own dark secret from the scrutiny of Mrs Lightowler.

True to his word, Lord Bulkeley was responsible for rigorous attempts to discover if any fugitives from Anglesey had reached the mainland on the night of the to-do, as some people called it. His men travelled as far as Conway, asking at every cottage along the shore, and in the villages of Llanfairfechan, and Penmaenmawr, but as they had no precise idea of how many people they were looking for, and whether men or women, they found no-one who had any information to impart. Search parties were also sent along the Anglesey shore, looking for bodies washed up on the strand or thrown onto the rocks, but the search uncovered nothing, and after a week it was called off.

Fishermen from Amlwch told the tale, in the Liverpool Arms, one night, a fortnight later, of a small tender which they had found floating in the open sea, a mile off Lynas Head. It could have come from anywhere, they agreed, given the recent mood of the tides and the winds, but the assertion by one, that it was stained with blood, was disputed by another, who accused his fellow of simply wishing to entertain the fireside company with a lurid tale. When they finished the tale by saying that, given the boat's poor state, and perhaps wishing to avoid bad luck, they had scuppered it and sent it to the bottom, there was a moment's thoughtful silence in the company, and then the busy din of the smoky parlour resumed.

Chapter 58

Jenna is sitting in the public records office at the University of North Wales, Bangor. Next to her is Professor William Dakin, an expert in genealogy, and before them, on the table, is a weighty leather-bound volume, with large, seemingly flimsy pages, containing lines of tiny and at first sight, seemingly illegible hieroglyphs. Phil and Rob, the technical crew, have set up their camera and microphones, and have already done a shot of Jenna and Professor Dakin, shaking hands and introducing themselves. A few feet away, just out of camera shot, is Maisie Flood.

On her return from America, Jenna slept, pretty well solidly, for twenty-four hours, and then began the process of getting her body clock back into synchronisation with London time. She was wondering whether or not to follow up her text to Maisie with another, trying to fix a lunch date, when the telephone rang, and it was Maisie herself.

"A break through," she announced.

"I hope this doesn't mean I've got to go back to the States!"

"Was it so bad? You poor thing. How was John?"

"Oh, he's a sweetie, really."

"Isn't he!" said Maisie, with a giggle. "Did he tell you all about his girlfriend?"

"Did he not!"

"Anyway, no. Nothing like that. This isn't your dad's family line, it's your mum's."

"Really?"

"Don't sound so surprised."

"No, it's just, I suppose people usually think of the male line first. Does that tell us something about the world!"

"Well, maybe, but it's the name, too, you know, continuity of the surname."

"Anyway, yes, so you've come up with something on my mum's side?"

"Yes. Shall we meet up in town. Is that OK?"

Jenna suppressed her curiosity in favour of a meeting.

"Shall we do lunch?"

"Sounds good."

"How are you for tomorrow?"

"I'm just pretending to have a look at my diary," said Maisie, with her usual little laugh, "but I know it's OK."

Jenna felt a wave of pure happiness inside. As soon as she had put the phone down, she began to decide what she was going to wear.

"I'm not going to tell you everything," said Maisie, at Grants. They had a table in the window, and Jenna had the agreeable feeling that everyone passing by was noticing them. "You're going to Anglesey, in Wales. We've found something about your mum's family that links them with a place there called Beaumaris."

"But you're not going to tell me what it is!"

"Not all of it. I want to see your reactions on the camera."

"Does that mean you're coming with me this time?"

"Yes," said Maisie, puckering her nose, in the way Jenna recalled from their first meeting, and once again she was perfectly happy to suppress her natural curiosity.

"What we already know, just from what your mother was able to tell us," said Professor Dakin, in his measured tone, "is that there was a family business in Shrewsbury which we've now been able to date back to the middle of the nineteenth century."

"Is this the pickle factory?"

"Well, not just pickles. That may have been a later speciality, but it was a time when the preservation of food was becoming a big industry. Remember, it was the high summer of the British Empire, ships were going out all over the world, and there was no proper refrigeration…"

"So, this would be foodstuff for export?"

"Export, yes, and for the domestic market. The technology was developing all the time, and your mother's forebears were somewhere there in the middle of it."

"So, how does it link up with Anglesey?"

"Well, bear with me a minute. The stroke of luck we had was that the name of the factory in Shrewsbury, was also a family name, and following that up in the census of 1851, which was when people had to start giving detailed information about the household and where they came from, we find a link with Beaumaris. Now if you look here…" Here the camera shot will show Jenna leaning forward to examine the page of the book on the table. "just here near the foot of the page, this is the record of a marriage which took place in Beaumaris in 1832."

Jenna screws her eyes tight to decipher the tiny scratchy writing. "Isobel Harcourt," she says, managing to draw the name into clarity.

"That's right. Isobel Harcourt."

"And is she my ancestor?"

"Yes."

"Isobel Harcourt. She sounds posh. Very English name. Was she from Anglesey?"

"No, we think she was probably a guest of Lord Bulkeley."

"Lord Bulkeley?"

"Yes. Very prestigious Anglesey family, even now."

"So, looking at this then," says Jenna, examining the rest of the marriage record, "she married beneath her, the naughty girl!"

"Well, you could say that."

"Thomas Coates," she enunciates, "Occupation, servant at Baron Hill. Baron Hill being…?"

"Lord Bulkeley's residence at Beaumaris."

"Right."

"And the name of the factory in Shrewsbury, going back to where we started…"

"Don't tell me. Coates?"

"That's right."

"But I don't ever remember there being a Coates side of the family."

"No, well you wouldn't. but if we look back to the 1851 census, we can see that Thomas and Isobel had four children, three boys and a girl. The girl, Charlotte, married Ralph Watson in 1850."

"And Watson's my mother's maiden name. Gosh, aren't you clever! So they were married, moved to Shrewsbury at some point and started a business and built a factory. Wouldn't they have needed some money to do that?"

"Presumably."

"He was a servant so it's unlikely he had any. So it must have been her money."

"Possibly. Though the records we have don't show us that, unfortunately."

"I think she fell madly in love with him and set him up in life. Not very romantic, though, is it, pickles!"

"Now," said Professor Dakin, moving one volume aside and drawing another into the line of the camera, "if we look at this other record, this line here shows Isobel's mother, who married twice…"

"So this person here would be her half-sister."

"Emily, yes. Now, if we go back further, we come to her grandfather, Edward Harcourt. At this stage it's very easy to get lost because family trees get a bit spidery after a while – if you think about it, say a family - one couple - have six kids, not uncommon in the past, that starts off six new branches, and if three of the children are girls, that's three new surnames, and not only are you starting a new branch of a family tree, you're joining it up with another one: it expands exponentially, and it can become a complete maze. The other thing that can happen, of course, is that it can just peter out altogether, but here we've had another bit of luck because Edward was High Sheriff of Devenham Castle in the early 1700s, which means that his name appears in various documents, and this means, to cut a long story short, that we can trace him back, through his mother's line, to this:

Sir Thomas Wilford, Idlington, b 1537
Mary Wilford, m
Anne Wilford, m [1]Sir Richard Bulkeley

"But isn't that…?"

"Yes, Sir Richard Bulkeley of Baron Hill, Beaumaris."

"Hang on a minute, so Isobel's great, great, what?"

"Aunt, I suppose, several greats to add!"

"So, Isobel's female ancestor was married to Sir Richard Bulkeley. So, presumably she would have known that when she came here as a guest."

"Well, not necessarily. It's nearly two hundred years and a lot of family branches have gone spinning off in their own direction since then, but the other thing you need to see is this. You see, Anne Wilford, or Anne Bulkeley was married twice."

"So is that what the [1] is in front of Sir Richard."

"Yes. And you'll see here, the [2] is someone called Thomas Cheadle."

"Right, and did they have any children?"

"Yes, but whether or not together is not known for certain. But what we do know is that the circumstances surrounding their relationship are somewhat murky. Thomas Cheadle became, Sir Thomas Cheadle, and played a role in events in Anglesey during the civil wars, but it was widely believed that Thomas and Anne had an adulterous relationship, and they were actually accused and tried for the murder of Sir Richard. There was certainly some kind of family feud which went on for some time, culminating in a duel between Sir Thomas' son, and Sir Richard's nephew, in which one was killed, and the other subsequently hanged for murder."

"Oh, my goodness, it sounds a bit like the Oresteia!"

"Well, we don't know for certain, but it seems likely that relations between the Wilfords and the Bulkeleys were somewhat cool."

"Frozen, I would have thought. So, it's quite possible that Isobel knew nothing about all this when she came here."

"Quite possible."

"But isn't it a bit of a coincidence?"

"Well, not necessarily. The circles which the Harcourts and the Bulkeleys moved in were not dissimilar, and by the early nineteenth century the Bulkeley family of Beaumaris had gone through some very significant modifications itself, so it's reasonable to assume that she could have come here as a guest without either her host or herself knowing that she was a distant relation of the Anne Wilford/Bulkeley/Cheadle who was the centre of all the controversy."

"So, I do have a skeleton in the family closet after all!"

"Bones rattling all over the place!"

"What happened to the other sister, Emily?"

"Well, there's also an Emily Harcourt in Shrewsbury in the 1851 census, which could well be her if we make the leap of thinking that she went to live near her sister."

"Did she have a family?"

"No. She's recorded as a spinster, living alone, apart from a housekeeper, and again in 1861, with the same housekeeper, now recorded as companion."

"I'm looking forward to seeing that played back," said Maisie, as they were winding up. "Lovely reactions on your face!"

"Gobsmacked! You could have warned me!"

"No, I couldn't."

"You did know though, didn't you, Maisie Flood? You knew the whole of my story, and you didn't tell me!"

"More than my job's worth, sweetie! We need to get some nice candid reactions, for the show."

"For the show. Long live the show. Vive la comedie!"

Maisie laughed, and for a moment, on the stairway of the central building of Bangor University, they twisted their fingers impulsively around each other's.

Chapter 59

"My God," said Jenna. "Just look at this place! I can't believe it."

Phil trains the camera on her face for a moment and then pans slowly round the scene.

From out of the thick tree foliage and the tangled undergrowth, emerges the ruined shell of a neo-classical mansion; the form still has some integrity, enough to suggest its former grandeur, but internally the process of ruination is complete. At one end of the building, through a ragged window slot, a series of ovens can be seen, set in the wall, obviously where the kitchens and the servants' quarters would once have been. At the other, broken timbers, and marks on the wall, indicate where once there was a great staircase, though the floors and ceilings throughout have largely subsided, leaving a chaos of rubble, laths and splintered timbers, with here a fragment of elaborately ornamented frieze, and there an upstairs door swinging open over a void.

They have been warned that it is dangerous to enter the building, and that even walking around the surrounds has its hazards.

For a time, as Phil completes his pan-shot, they stand absolutely still and silent, Jenna, Maisie, Rob, and Ryan Hughes, the expert from the Antiquarian Society who is their guide.

Then, they begin to organise the shoot. Mr Hughes explains that the Bulkeley family moved from Baron Hill in the 1920s, to more modest accommodation not far away, because of death duties after the first war, and the prohibitive cost of the building's upkeep as a dwelling. It was used as a store for some time; then, during the second war, Polish soldiers were billeted there, and a fire which went out of control created widespread damage. Since then, he says, the building has been abandoned, leaving nature to spread its confusion, now evident in the dank undergrowth, the thick trunked ivy, the wild bushes, and the overarching trees.

He shows them some photographs of the house and gardens as they were in the late nineteenth and early twentieth century, amongst them one which shows the King, Edward the seventh, taking tea with the family on the terrace outside the house, in 1907, when he came to open the University of Bangor. The spot where they sit at the table is now covered by a wild thorn bush, but the aspect of the photograph is still clearly recognisable, the great bowed window behind, the stone stairway with balustrade to the right leading down to what were once formal gardens but now a wilderness of unkempt growth.

"OK, Jenna, if you could just improvise, you know, reactions to being here, that kind of thing?"

"I'm trying to get my head around the fact," Jenna begins, "that at two different points, two hundred years apart, two of my ancestors were here, actually here, and now it's a ruin. A complete ruin. And once it must have been so beautiful. Very sad."

"OK, that'll do. We'll put the rest together later."

Phil and Rob are anxious to get the equipment back to the car, which they have left parked awkwardly by the road, before the rain, already pattering through the leaves, comes on too heavily. Jenna shakes hands with Mr Hughes, and he takes his leave.

"Are you coming guys?" Phil calls to Jenna and Maisie, who are still lingering by the house.

"It's Ok, we'll walk."

"It's raining, darling."

"Don't care."

"Well, don't be long. Want to be on the road by one."

"Look, why don't you go on without us," said Maisie.

She looked at Jenna, and they exchanged a brief almost business-like nod.

"We'll stay on. Make a weekend of it. Catch the train back, Monday."

"You sure?"

"Mmm."

"OK, lovebirds. Leave you to it."

"Did I just hear what I think I heard?" asks Jenna.

"Mmm."

"Did you know this bit of my story, too, Maisie Flood?"

"I told you sometimes there are unexpected outcomes. That's the fun of it."

"I wonder if the other sister came here, too."

"Emily. The one with the housekeeper."

"Housekeeper-stroke-companion. What do you make of it

"Same-sex couple?"

"Yes, I was wondering that."

They both laughed, then, with just the sound of the rain pattering softly but now steadily through the leaves of the high surrounding trees, they walked, hand in hand around the crumbling mansion to the terrace which had once stood above the beautiful formal gardens of Baron Hill.

It was a truly magical moment.

Chapter 60

"Just look at that," said Maisie, sitting by the window in her blue silk kimono, pulling the curtain of the room wide enough for Jenna to see. A thin wraith of mist lay over the Menai Strait, and the first aura of dawn, from beyond the slate black mountain sent colours of pink and turquoise and gold and magenta into the surrounding air and over the limpid water.

"It's beautiful," said Maisie. "I don't think I've ever seen anything so beautiful."

They had checked in for a further two nights at the Bulkeley Hotel. Two delicious days together in the lovely early summer rain.

"Come back to bed," said Jenna, gesturing towards her across the wide room.

"I was going to make you some coffee."

"I don't want coffee."

Maisie turned and smiled.

Jenna beckoned with her hand.

Maisie stood and moved slowly back towards the bed.

"Can I tell you a secret?" she said, sitting on the side of the bed.

"If you like."

"It's a confession."

Jenna smiled, though something inside told her that she didn't want confessions. She didn't want complications; she only wanted things to be as simple as they had been since the moment in the abandoned garden of Baron Hill, with the fresh smell of vegetation released in the early summer rain.

"Go on, then, confess!"

"When I was twelve, I fell in love with Swatch. All my friends were crazy about Switch but I fell madly in love with Swatch, and that's how I knew…"

"You poor thing!" said Jenna, remembering that she had said that to Maisie once before, and feeling slightly old.

By the time they went down for breakfast, the beauty of the dawn had been overtaken by another wave of rain, serried ranks of cloud that came from the mountains whose clearly defined ridges and summits were now swathed in mist.

The rain eased for an hour in the afternoon, and they walked from the Green at Beaumaris onto the high ground which looked one way back to the castle, and the other over the strait towards the Lavan Sands, now emerging from the low tide. But already a little bit of the magic was gone.

They had a meal at the hotel's restaurant; the food was only adequate and it was Sunday evening, so there was no-one else in the room, no atmosphere. In the room, they plugged into each other's i-pod. Jenna chose the Adagio from Mahler's Fifth to share with Maisie. She wanted her to be as moved as she was, to be taken into that world of sublime emotions, but when she looked at Maisie's face, she seemed indifferent, still reading her *HELLO* magazine, as she tended to do when listening to her own music.

"I just find it a bit boring," Maisie said, when asked.

"What sort of music does your friend in Kingston like?"

It was the wrong question to ask.

Maisie's face took on a look that was stubborn, and stupid, and refractory.

And Jenna felt silently angry and resentful. So typical, to dismiss things without making any effort at all.

They avoided the argument but they both knew. And just as if there had been an argument with regrettable things said that couldn't be unsaid, the damage was done.

"I just feel that you're stifling me."

Not Maisie's words, but her own, to Eleanor, nine years ago.

They slept together, but only because it would have been more awkward not to. Jenna got up at six, showered and then made

Maisie a cup of coffee. Then she went down to breakfast alone, not because she was hungry, but because she wanted to be alone.

They took a taxi to the station at Bangor. Then a train to Chester, and a connection to London.

And that, as Jenna knew, was that.

Chapter 61

Two weeks later, a cheque came through, via Bex, who called to confirm its arrival.

"I didn't expect it so quickly," she told Bex.

"Simon's usually pretty good. So, I take it it's all wrapped up, then?"

"I think so. Haven't heard anything for a while, anyway."

"I've got some provisional schedules through for *Country Retreats*. Shall I fax them or do you want to pick them up?"

"I'll call in," said Jenna.

"Perhaps we can have lunch."

Putting the phone down, she felt a little touch of sadness, remembering the last time she had been to lunch, at Grants.

And then, almost immediately, the telephone rang again, and it was Maisie. The sound of her voice caused Jenna an involuntary rush of mixed sensations, not least amongst which was that of anguished expectation.

It was, however, business. They had come across a portrait of Isobel Harcourt at the Villiers Institute and Simon thought it might be a good idea to set something up.

"You don't have to, we can just get some piccies and cut them in, it's up to you, really."

Jenna imagined Maisie wrinkling her nose at this, the way she did.

"No, I can be there. I'd like to see what she looked like," she replied. She resisted the temptation to ask Maisie if she would be there, too.

Phil was there, and John, who nodded to her and smiled, in what might almost have been a knowing wink. Phil briefed her about the paintings and they spent twenty minutes discussing the 'script', though, as with *Country Retreats*, nothing was written down. Then, she was ready to begin, waiting for John and Simon to give her the nod.

I'm sitting in this room at the Villiers Institute, and I'm looking at a portrait of my ancestor, Isobel Harcourt. The portrait was painted by an artist called James Pennington, and it depicts a well-to-do young lady, in a green gown, with a black chapeau and feather, and gloves in her hand, who looks as if she might be going out riding. There are two other paintings, one is of another young lady wearing the same costume, and the other is of a rather proud-looking youth, though a closer look soon tells you that the youth and the young lady are one and the same person. This person has been identified, from paintings by other artists of the time, as Meg Liddle, a girl who modelled, probably for very little payment to supplement whatever income she had from other, possibly, dubious sources!

What is strange to me, besides the fact of looking directly at a representation of my ancestor, is that these are the only three works that survived of the artist, James Pennington. All we know of him besides is from a series of references unearthed in the diary of a contemporary, Christopher Ford, a bookseller and would-be poet. The diary is very sketchy, it has to be said, most of the references being like this for July 1831, supped with Pennington at Cutlers *or this from September of the same year* supped with Pennington and talked late. *When we come to November, however, we find this,* No sign yet of Pennington, I fear he has done what he promised. *And that, somewhat cryptic note, is the last. Whatever Pennington promised to do, or whether or not he did it, we have no way of knowing. What seems to be the case is that he disappeared and was heard of no more, leaving only these three paintings, one of them of my ancestor, Isobel Harcourt, to the world. Whether the paintings are good or not – they're good enough to be here, I suppose – I really don't know, I'm no art critic, but what strikes me most in all three paintings are the eyes of the subject, and in all three Pennington seems to have captured a look of both yearning and gladness that, to me, anyway, is an expression of love.*

"And close-up of the eyes of Isobel," said Phil, "and cut. Thanks Jenna, that was great. We may well not have time to include all that in the cut, but we'll see how it goes."

"Thanks, Phil. Is that it?"

"That's it. Simon's overseeing the final edit. Probably be able to let you have a download in a couple of weeks. I expect Maisie will give you a call."

"Yes, right," said Jenna, "thanks."

Maisie, of course, was not there.

At first she had felt a pang of disappointment; in spite of herself, she had pictured being able to go out for a coffee afterwards, half an hour, perhaps, rescue a few bits of something. But no, she was not there, and it was, all things considered, thought Jenna, just as well.

Chapter 62

Roger Harcourt's coach was making progress through the busy market place on Jennyfield Lane, when the door of the coach opened, and a young man, carrying a carpet bag, quickly pulled himself up from the step and then sat opposite him. Harcourt's first instinct, for audacious robberies in open public places were by no means a rarity, was to pick up his cane, bang it on the roof so that Ezra Lightowler would hear it, and then use it to bring the young fellow a couple of swift blows across the head. That he did not do so is to be explained by the fact that, as his initial shock subsided - for it all took place in an instant - he recognised the young man who sat facing him.

"Daniel Flynn!" he muttered.

"At your service," the fellow replied, with a slight inclination of the head.

"Not at my service, you scoundrel! Not any more!"

"What wrong did I do, apart from ensuring that your ward did not fall into the trap you set for her?"

"What wrong? How much did he pay you?"

"He paid me nothing, but I paid dearly and I have come to settle the account."

"You'll get no money out of me. Not you, not him, nor yet the little whore you used as a decoy for my niece."

"There was no decoy," said Daniel, now taking off his hat and allowing his hair, stacked up inside it, to tumble down onto his shoulders. Next he took off his topcoat, and put it into his carpetbag, and Roger Harcourt watched, transfixed, as the transformation became complete. "No decoy," repeated Meg Liddle. "Why pay someone else when you can do the job yourself?"

"Has he put you up to this? Where is he?"

"I have a message for you from him."

"Where is he?"

"Where you may soon find him yourself."

"What message?"

"That is the message," said Meg, reaching into the carpetbag and drawing out the small silver pistol with which Robert Pennington had once threatened to end his own life.

The shot which Ezra Lightowler heard, and which made him stop the horse, and sit bolt still, was undoubtedly of such loudness and nearness that it could only have come from within the coach. It was a knowledge, however, his instinct told him, that could later be denied. *I just heard a shot, and stopped the horse, I didn't know where it came from, it could have been from anywhere.* He already heard himself saying this, and he was pretty sure no-one would question it.

His instinct continued to prompt him, for, as a man who knew which side his bread was buttered on, he had an instinct which was as quick and sure-footed as a mountain goat. The sound having definitely come from inside the coach, the great likelihood was that someone had been shot. Now, if someone was desperate enough to shoot his master, that person might also be desperate enough to shoot anyone else who might be a witness of that, and what better way of avoiding being a witness than to sit bolt still and see nothing? If his master had been shot, the likelihood was that he, Ezra Lightowler, would be forced to look for alternative employment; if on the other hand, it was his master who had done the shooting, the likelihood was that his master would be hanged, in which case also, he, Ezra Lightowler, would be forced to look for alternative employment. It was very much to be regretted, either way, but there was nothing to be done about it, and since he could not influence events, it suited Ezra Lightowler to sit bolt still and see nothing.

Roger Harcourt was discovered, sitting in the corner of his coach with an expression in his open eyes, which, were it not for the small red hole in his forehead, might have been taken for simple astonishment. In the crowd which quickly gathered around the coach, there were two or three who could vouch that they had seen a young man entering the coach at the other end of the market. In the confusion that followed the sound of the shot, there was no-one who had seen a young man departing the coach, though Meg Liddle, who by now had joined the crowd, told the constable that she had seen such a young man running so fast through Vinegar Gardens that he had almost knocked her down.

"If we catch him, you'll have to be a witness," said the constable.

"That I will," said Meg Liddle.

The constable turned his attention to the driver of the coach.

"I just heard a shot, and stopped the horse," said the driver. "I didn't know where it came from, it could have been from anywhere."

Chapter 63

In the aftermath of the civil war, the castles of Wales, once strongholds of the English over the Welsh, were rendered unfit ever again to be strongholds of rebellion. This was the fate of Beaumaris and Conway; it was also the fate of Aberlleiniog, and Thomas Cheadle, now increasingly beset by ill health, began to live a retired life, with his wife, Anne, in the farmhouse at Lleiniog, on the coast, half a mile distant from the rampart.

It was some time before Richard could be persuaded to leave the island and seek his fortune elsewhere. Gradually, however, as he saw old age settling on his father and his step mother, he came to accept that the island of Anglesey held no future for him. Preparations were made, and on a certain day, in January 1650, Thomas Cheadle accompanied his son to the ferry at Llanfaes, just as, nearly thirty years before, he had accompanied Sir Richard Bulkeley.

A mist, which had obscured the mainland coast since dawn was now beginning to lift under a pale winter sun, and the Lavan Sands, emerging from the falling tide, ran into the distance.

"It will be a good day for travelling," said Thomas Cheadle. "You'll get to Chester by nightfall. You know what to do when you reach Liverpool."

"Yes, father."

"Good luck, then."

"I'll send word."

"God speed."

The young man hugged his father briefly then quickly turned to go. Thomas watched as he mounted the ferry boat, his heart heavy with the sorrow of parting. But he was glad for the boy;

the world would be open before him.

It was just when the ferry had reached the midway point, that Thomas Cheadle, looking towards the landward shore, saw another horseman approaching, intending, no doubt, to meet the ferry and cross to the island. By the time he recognised the colours of Sir Richard Bulkeley, Anne's nephew, it was too late to call the ferry back.

"Quickly," he called to the ferryman's boy, who was standing idly by awaiting his master's return. "Push that skiff into the water and row me across."

"But…"

"Do it!"

Too frightened to argue, the lad did as he'd been told. Richard Cheadle, by now, was just dismounting onto the sands, with his horse, but had not seen the other horseman approaching, now less than a hundred yards from him.

Thomas Cheadle shouted, using every ounce of his ageing strength to fill the air with his stark warning. Richard looked up, and for a moment stood with a puzzled look, and then, hearing the approaching hooves, turned to see the reason for his father's alarm.

Cheadle watched from the boat, and though he could not hear the words, he read the taunts on Bulkeley's lips. His son turned away, busying himself with his own horse's girth, and Cheadle willed him to mount and simply ride away. The very act of ignoring his tormentor, however, had the effect of making him redouble his jibes, and there came a moment when Richard Cheadle turned and drew his sword.

"No!" shouted Cheadle, for he was certain that his son was no match for Sir Richard Bulkeley.

It was too late.

Dismounting, Bulkeley now drew his own sword, and the two men faced each other with their points. There followed two or three harmless passes, and to any observer, it might have seemed that Sir Richard Bulkeley was toying with his young opponent. Then Cheadle saw his son attempt a lunge, and, surprised, Bulkeley had to step back and parry; from that moment, it began to have the complexity of a real fencing match, with the full array of stroke and counterstroke that both men had been taught so well.

The boat was now just a few yards away, and Thomas Cheadle called again, but the two men, caught up in the heat of their rivalry, ignored him. It was only by physically intervening between them, Cheadle reasoned, that he could put a stop to it, and this, as he stepped out of the boat into the shallow water of the bank, was what he intended to do.

His son, now aware of his presence, looked up, and it was this moment, as he let his concentration slip, that his opponent chose to make a sudden lunge. As he did so, however, his footing slipped in the give of the sand, and stumbling forward, the force of his own weight took him onto the defensive parry of his opponent's blade.

He fell to the ground, struggled for a moment as if to get up and avenge his embarrassment, and then dropped suddenly into a lifeless stillness.

The point of the blade had pierced his heart.

Richard Cheadle dropped his sword to the ground, in horror. There was terror in his eyes.

His father held him, to steady the shaking, and ran his fingers through his hair.

The boy, he knew, had put his head into a noose.

Chapter 64

"Congratulations!" said Bex.

Jenna feigned surprise though she had known full well that the show was going out and had already spoken to her mum at length.

The edit was miraculous. Even the American fiasco had been rendered as an interesting five-minute short story. And it was, just as Maisie had said, the facial expressions, the moments of surprise, of taking things in, that made it. That was the way it worked.

"Anyway, listen, good news, I've had Stephen Bligh on the phone this morning. He wants to know if you're available in November and December."

"What for?"

"If I were to say the word 'jungle', would that mean anything?"

"Now you really are joking! Not…"

"The very same. *I'm a celebrity…*"

There was a moment's pause and then they both chimed in together at the top of their voices: *Get me out of here!!!*

Chapter 65

There had been a cemetery at Lowfield for as long as anyone could remember, growing each year so much that it seemed it would become as large as the city itself, whose occupants it so hungrily devoured. The oldest legible inscriptions, apart from those protected from the weather inside crypts, went back two centuries, but others, rounded and formless, bore witness to a tradition whose origin was lost in the mists of time. Chronicles in the present church, itself a mere three hundred years old, might record evidence of Anglo-Saxon, or, before that, Celtic burial rituals, but it was generally believed that it had never been anything else but a place of burial, perhaps even that during the six days of his great labour, God had set aside this piece of land for a purpose which, in the remit of newly created time, he knew would be most necessary.

Emily Harcourt, standing at the open grave of her guardian, Roger Harcourt, listened to the minister completing, as by a dull rote, the words of the funeral service, and then turned to thank the people who had joined the gathering to pay their respects. It was not a duty which promised to occupy her long. Mr Mobbes, the old manservant, Mrs Livesey, the cook, two or three gentlemen who announced themselves as members of his club, and the minister himself. Isobel, of course, was not there.

As the gathering dispersed, following the minister towards the old wrought iron gates where their coaches were waiting, Emily looked one last time at the grave and then, looking up, saw the girl again.

It might have seemed a coincidence that Meg Liddle should be returning from a visit to her grandmother's grave, at the same time that Roger Harcourt's cortege was making its way from his newly prepared dwelling, but a coincidence it was not. She had been a regular visitor to Lowfield cemetery for the last week, attempting to pacify a certain resident who had been going in for a vigorous bout of turning, and she had made it her business to know when the Harcourt funeral was to take place.

She had watched the proceedings from a distance, safe from view behind a hawthorn tree, and now that the guests were leaving, she felt an obligation to wait until Emily, too, had departed, before leaving herself. And it was at that moment that their eyes met.

She was a pretty girl, Emily noted, as she approached, though her clothes were a little shabby, and she looked unhappy; it was the eyes, however, that intrigued her most, because they were eyes that belonged to someone else, and she knew who that person was.

"You were Daniel, weren't you?"

The girl nodded.

"What's your proper name?"

"Meg."

"Why did you come to Beaumaris?"

"I followed him. Mr Pennington, that is. Robert. I loved him."

Emily nodded, and certain pieces of the puzzle fell into place.

"And you turned yourself into a boy."

"I'm an artist's model. I turn myself into all kinds of things."

"What happened, on that night?"

"I took your sister's things. I suppose you know that. We were only meant to go as far as the ferry and then show your guardian up for the fool he was. But they had guns. There was a boat. James knew where it was, We tried to row out of range but he was caught in the neck. I managed to get him out of the boat, onto the sands, but he was bleeding a lot. He died in my arms. I sat with him as long as I could, but then the water came up and I had to leave him."

"I'm sorry."

"I found refuge in a fisherman's cottage at a place called Morfa

Madryn. The old woman looked after me and kept me hidden when they came looking. I realised they hadn't found his body."

"No. They searched. For both of you. But Thomas – you remember Thomas – says the tides and currents are unpredictable at this season. A body could be taken anywhere. And they didn't even know if there was a body."

"It's better that way. I don't think he'd like to be in a place like this."

"No," said Emily, ruefully.

"I'm sorry about your guardian."

"He wasn't a good man. His coachman told us things about him, things he'd been forced to keep secret. To my shame, I paid him the money he asked to keep silent. I know it's wrong, but Isobel is going to be married soon, and I didn't want the family name mixed up with any more gossip or scandal."

"She's getting married?"

"Yes. She's marrying Thomas."

"Thomas?"

"Yes."

Meg smiled, a smile that conveyed a million thoughts. "It was me who killed him, you know," she said at last. "I knew I'd never get justice there, so I decided to get justice here, myself. You can tell them, if you like."

"I've already told them."

"Told them what?"

"That it was Daniel Flynn who killed my guardian. A man they'll never find."

"Thank you. I wish another person not far from here would be as understanding."

"Who's that?"

"My grandmother. She's buried here, too."

Emily nodded and smiled. They walked towards the gate, from which, all the coaches but Emily's had now departed.

"You'll find someone else," she said.

"No. I've lost the man I love. I'll never love another."

"I too lost the man I love. And I too will never love another man."

They reached the cemetery gates.

"What will you do?"

"I don't know. I was a model for the artists, as I told you, but I have no will to do that again."

"I'm going to live near Isobel, when she moves to Shrewsbury after the wedding."

"That's nice."

"I shall need a housekeeper, if you would be interested."

"I don't know."

"Will you think about it?"

"I don't know. It's just…"

"I'm staying at Evesham Place for three days. Come and see me there and tell me your decision."

"It's just that I don't know if I would make a very good housekeeper."

Emily thought for a moment and then smiled. "Say a companion, then."

Chapter 66

The journey to Conway was arduous for a man of obvious infirmity, and his elderly wife. They seemed a couple who should be at home, seeing out their days in front of a warm fire, not travelling to this, the most dreadful of vigils.

When they brought him into the yard, the boy's face was pale as if he had seen no proper light for weeks. His eyes squinted in the harsh winter sun.

"I loved him as if he were my own," said Anne Cheadle, her voice harsh with suppressed tears.

"I know."

They put the rope around his neck.

"Stop them, stop them!" cried Anne, helplessly.

A gang of labourers, at work dismantling the rampart, stopped and looked up at the critical moment, sniggering as the protest of the dangling body became a twitching dance.

Then it was over.

THE END

Thank you for reading this book. Please leave a review or a rating on Amazon. If you have enjoyed it, and would like to read other books by John Wheatley, please see the following:

Other John Wheatley titles set in Anglesey

FLOWERS OF VITRIOL

https://www.amazon.co.uk/Flowers-Vitriol-John-Wheatley-ebook/dp/B005HC6EYW

It is 1817 and on the streets of Amlwch, the copper capital of the world, discontent amongst the poor, the hungry and the disaffected, is about to break out into open violence. Mine Superintendent, Thomas Kendrick, brings his bride, the beautiful Cornish girl, Alys, twenty years his junior, home to Amlwch. The arrival of the Irish sea captain, and his friendship with Kendrick, sets off an intriguing tale of love, jealousy, treachery and blackmail...

THE WEEPING SANDS

https://www.amazon.co.uk/Weeping-Sands-John-Wheatley-ebook/dp/B005RO8GNM

The Weeping Sands is a captivating historical saga interweaving four tales of love and loss through four centuries in the life of Baron Hill, Anglesey's ancestral mansion.

Jenna Shaw, 32, children`s TV presenter, is invited to take part in a TV show exploring her ancestry, a quest which will take her, ultimately, to the ruined mansion of Baron Hill, in Beaumaris, Anglesey. 350 years earlier, Thomas Cheadle, despised for his affair with Lady Anne Bulkeley, and blamed for the death of her husband, prepares to play his part as the Civil War reaches Wales. Isobel Harcourt, recovering from a breakdown following a failed love affair with artist, James Pennington, and in the protection of her sister, is taken to Beaumaris, Anglesey, to convalesce. The year is 1831.

How do Isobel`s strange delusions link the past and the present? What will be the outcome of Jenna`s quest?

THE PAPERS OF MATTHEW LOCKE

https://www.amazon.co.uk/Papers-Matthew-Locke-John-Wheatley-ebook/dp/B007KAYC20

When Matthew Locke survives a shipwreck on the coast of Anglesey, he is cared for by the family of Llyws Llewellyn in the fishing village of Rhosneigr. During his recovery from the ordeal, he finds himself slipping through boundaries of time, becoming involved in events from Anglesey`s mysterious past. In these episodes, he meets, in different guises, Bryony, Llwys Llewellyn`s elder daughter, and it is here that their strange love affair begins.

Set in Anglesey in the 1880s, and beginning with the loss of `The Norman Court`, a clipper in the Java sugar trade, John Wheatley`s novel explores the shadowy territory between history, myth and fantasy.

THE EXILE'S DAUGHTER

https://www.amazon.co.uk/Exile-Daughter-John-Wheatley-ebook/dp/B00AB4BFXG

When Lauren Bucievski and her father take flight from Poland during the 1905 revolution, the ten year old girl has little understanding of who her father`s enemies are. Seven years later, when she befriends the happy-go-lucky Jimmy Jilkes, and when the charismatic Stefan turns up from Poland, her life is thrown into conflict, vulnerable as she is, in her isolation, to her own dawning sexuality. The outbreak of war in 1914 becomes the defining factor in how each of their destinies will turn out.

Also by JOHN WHEATLEY

ENOCH'S HAMMER

Set in 1812,`Enoch`s Hammer` follows the story of the so-called Luddites of Yorkshire from their first major uprising in February 1812 to the mass trial at York in January 1813 which led to multiple hangings and transportations. It focuses on the three men who were hanged for the murder of William Horsfall, an industrialist, George Mellor, William Thorpe and Thomas Smith, and makes an imaginative reconstruction of their personal and private lives. The other major characters are Joseph Radcliffe, the Magistrate of Milnsbridge House, who was obsessive in hunting down the Luddites and making convictions, John Lloyd, a solicitor who brought new and devious techniques to the art of interrogation, and Lieutenant General the Hon. George Maitland who co-ordinated the military effort to suppress the Luddite movement, and who co-ordinated the York trials.

https://www.amazon.co.uk/dp/B07VSCDDLK

JOHN WHEATLEY' MIDDLETON NOVELS

MARCIA

Set in the town of Middleton, to the north of Manchester, MARCIA tells the story of a first love that continues to haunt two people long after their lives have gone in different directions. Recording the rituals and intimacies of courtship and marriage, the novel evokes the changing faces of Middleton through four decades as it moves towards its post-industrial present.

https://www.amazon.co.uk/Marcia-John-Wheatley-ebook/dp/B00C1426Z0

EVELYN

John Wheatley`s second Middleton novel takes us back to the second world war and its impact on two Middleton families. Evelyn and Maureen, sisters-in-law, are drawn together when their husbands go away to serve. For Evelyn, the idyllic pre-war early years of her marriage are replaced the darkness and loneliness of separation. Both young women face conflicts and temptations, and in the aftermath of the war, both have hard decisions to make as they try to rebuild their lives.

https://www.amazon.co.uk/Evelyn-John-Wheatley-ebook/dp/B00FKH1YP8

CANKY'S TRADE

Canky`s Trade` is set in the south Lancashire township of Middleton in 1811. Lord Byron, pursuing a legal entitlement which he had in nearby Rochdale, stayed at Hopwood Hall, close to Middleton in September of 1811, and the novel deals partly with Byron`s impact on the people he meets there. And it was in the middle of the period when Oliver Canky, sexton of the parish churchyard, plied his `trade`. Throw in a young local weaver and poet, Sam Bamford, a murdered prostitute and some strange goings on in the cellar of the isolated house of Canky`s friend, `Owd Scrat`, and there you have the basic ingredients of this darkly comic story....

https://www.amazon.co.uk/dp/B00G70KY7G

JOSS

When she is displaced to Middleton, near Manchester, England, in 1962, to stay with her strange Aunt Mary, an unhappy 13-year-old Joanna Logan, begins a diary. The diary reflects all her unanswered questions about what is happening with her parents. It also records her experience of Middleton, and the friendship she forms with Joss, the boy from down the street, who, unknown to his family, is keeping a special dog, Riverside Lad. Twenty-five years later, Joanna returns to Middleton, and discovers the secrets which lay beneath her aunt`s life, secrets which she never suspected at the time.

https://www.amazon.co.uk/dp/B07HB9NWR5

CONSEQUENCES

How will Tony cope with life after serving a prison sentence for a manslaughter he did not commit? Why did he plead guilty? Is there someone he tried to protect? The story begins with a perfect holiday romance between Tony and Jenny. The relationship is intense but also poisoned by jealousy, and a fight at a party between Tony and Ben leads to him being the obvious suspect when Ben's body is later found. Tony describes his prison experience and his attempts to rehabilitate himself when he is released eight years later. He spends some time in Spain, with his widowed stepmother, who helps to rescue him from his self-destructive mind-set. Finally, he returns to the UK to find Jenny. What will happen when he confronts her with the truth of that night at the party? What, if anything, can be rescued of their relationship?

Set in Middleton, in the north-west of England, in the 80s and 90s.

https://www.amazon.co.uk/dp/B097Z1NBBN

FINDING JOSIE – A second Chance Romance

https://www.amazon.co.uk/dp/finding-Josie-john-wheatley/dp/B07VSCDDLK

When Nick Roberts returns to Middleton for the funeral of an old friend, he is haunted by memories of the good times they shared, and of Josie, his first love, who was so much a part of it all. Finding Josie now, in the few days he has left in Middleton, her becomes his obsession. But where might she be, now, and how might she have changed with the years? And where will Nick's search lead him? To a second chance romance, or to love's final disappointment? And where, he wonders. for starters, will the search even begin?

IDLERS CORNER: A Tale of the Great Middleton Flood of 1927

July 1927. After months of rain, the canal embankment a mile above Middleton collapses sending millions of gallons of filthy water cascading down on the town leaving destruction in its wake. How will the town cope with this catastrophe? And how will Maggie Clayton, 20, a carder at the Neva Mill, cope with the consequences of finding herself alone, on the day of the flood, with Danny Beswick, a bright spark of a lad whose intentions are not always honourable?

https://www.amazon.co.uk/dp/B0D9Q4Q7LL

IDLERS RETURN

How will Maggie cope when the father of her child returns after abandoning her five years before?

IDLERS RETURN continues the saga of the Clayton family. It is now 1932 five years after the Middleton Flood, with the two sisters Maggie and Annie both married though in very different circumstances. The town itself is suffering economic hardship and the threat of redundancy and short-time working hangs over the heads of many of the workforce.

Tom, Maggie's brother, has now joined the police force and is engaged to Helen who has had to to take on work in a pub, The Commercial. It is here that she comes across Danny Beswick, who, unbeknown to her or Tom, is the father of Maggie's little girl, Rosie.
Will Danny's return be harmless, or will it become the catalyst to expose the cracks in the Clayton family's relationships?

https://www.amazon.co.uk/dp/B0DJTCV5RY

MIDDLETON DAYS

These stories, partly fictional, partly biographical, reflect the Middleton I grew up in during the fifties and sixties. Though only a few miles from Manchester, Middleton still thought of itself as an independent 'cotton' town, and mills and factory chimneys dominated the landscape. My teenage years corresponded with the emergence of the Beatles and pop culture, and that influenced us all a lot, and it was during those years that Middleton really changed, too.

https://www.amazon.co.uk/dp/B09MV4PF8D

ABOUT THE AUTHOR

John Wheatley was born and brought up in Middleton in the 1950s and 1960s. He has written a number of novels with settings in Anglesey, Middleton and Yorkshire.

They are all available as kindle e-books from AMAZON. Paperbacks can also be bought from AMAZON **or directly from John by sending an email to:**

johnwheatley@ymail.com

He would love to hear from you for a chat.

You can also follow 'John Wheatley Author' on Facebook and have a chat there, if you like.

Printed in Great Britain
by Amazon